Praise for *Adventures of a Dwergish Girl*

"*Adventures of A Dwergish Girl* is a book with every single thing I love about Pinkwater novels."
—Cory Doctorow, author of *Little Brother*

"Pinkwater is arguably Pratchett-for-kids, Wodehouse-for-new-millennium-juniors. Or, if you like, Rocky and Bullwinkle in written form, with equally zany illustrations . . . This book is just so darned nice that it could cure your whole day."
—*Green Man Review*

"Captivating, cool and crazy! This story is an inspiration to us all: Be brave. Have adventures. And, most importantly, follow your dreams."
—Sam Lloyd, author of *Mr. Pusskins*

"With touches of magic, conversations with ghosts, and a dash of danger in the form of gold-stealing gangsters, *Adventures of a Dwergish Girl* is sure to delight."
—Alane Adams, author of the Legends of Orkney series

"Richly-drawn, quirky, and mysterious, Daniel Pinkwater's *Adventures of a Dwergish Girl* pulls readers into a dazzling adventure, complete with android Redcoats, urban magic, and of course, the

very best pizza New York City has to offer."
—Susan Vaught, author of *Footer Davis Probably Is Crazy*

"*Adventures of a Dwergish Girl* by Daniel Pinkwater has that rare sense of wonder that makes you feel as if you have entered into a magical kingdom."
—Joe R. Lansdale, author of *Of Mice and Minestrone*

"Highly recommended. I'm going to buy a hard copy when it's published so I can throw it at my nephew when he's old enough to appreciate it."
—*Welcome to Camp Telophase*

Daniel Pinkwater

Adventures of a Dwergish Girl

Other titles by Daniel Pinkwater

Young Adult
Wingman (1975)
Lizard Music (1976)
The Last Guru (1978)
Alan Mendelsohn, Boy From Mars (1979)
Yobgorgle: Mystery Monster of Lake Ontario (1979)
The Worms of Kukumlima (1981)
The Snarkout Boys and the Avocado of Death (1982)
Young Adult Novel (1982)
The Snarkout Boys and the Baconburg Horror (1984)
Borgel (1990)
The Education of Robert Nifkin (1998)
The Neddiad: How Neddie Took the Train, Went to Hollywood, and Saved Civilization (2007)
The Yggyssey (2009)
The Adventures of a Cat-Whiskered Girl (2010)
Bushman Lives! (2012)

Series
The Hoboken Chicken Emergency
The Hoboken Chicken Emergency (1977)
Looking for Bobowicz: A Hoboken Chicken Story (2004)
The Artsy Smartsy Club (2005)

Magic Moscow
The Magic Moscow (1980)
Attila the Pun: A Magic Moscow Story (1981)
Slaves of Spiegel: A Magic Moscow Story (1982)

Mrs. Noodlekugel
Mrs. Noodlekugel (2012)
Mrs. Noodlekugel and Four Blind Mice (2013)
Mrs. Noodlekugel and Drooly the Bear (2015)

The Werewolf Club
The Magic Pretzel (2000)
The Lunchroom of Doom (2000)
The Werewolf Club Meets Dorkula (2001)
The Hound of the Basketballs (2001)
The Werewolf Club Meets Oliver Twit (2002)

Collections
Young Adults (1991)
5 Novels (1997)
4 Fantastic Novels (2000)
Once Upon a Blue Moose (2006)

Adventures
of a
Dwergish
Girl

Daniel
Pinkwater

Tachyon
San Francisco

Adventures of a Dwergish Girl
Copyright 2020 © Daniel Pinkwater

Cover art by Aaron Renier
Cover design by Elizabeth Story
Interior illustration by Aaron Renier
Interior design by Elizabeth Story

Tachyon Publications LLC
1459 18th Street #139
San Francisco, CA 94107
415.285.5615
www.tachyonpublications.com
tachyon@tachyonpublications.com

Series Editor: Jacob Weisman
Project Editor: Jill Roberts

Print ISBN: 978-1-61696-336-1
Digital ISBN: 978-1-61696-337-8

First Edition: 2020

10 9 8 7 6 5 4 3 2 1

1.

There are places in the Catskill Mountains you cannot find. It doesn't matter
if you are a forest ranger, an Eagle Scout,
a Native American tracker, or the president
of the Sierra Club, you can get close to the
places I'm telling about, but you can't get to
them because you can't find them. I can get
to them. I can walk right up to them, and go
inside them. That's because I grew up there,
and my people have lived in those spots for
hundreds and hundreds of years.

I am not an American Indian. Not a member of the Munsee Esopus tribe of the Lenape

nation or the Minisink tribe either. In fact the native people never lived in the Catskills up to about the year 1790. They'd go there to fish and hunt, or pass through on the way to someplace else, but they didn't make permanent settlements in the actual mountains, for some reason or other. I'll come back to that in a little while.

The Catskill Mountains are big, close to six thousand square miles, they cover five counties, and they're part of the Appalachian Mountains, but they're not huge like the Rockies or the whole Appalachian chain, so they're not particularly unexplorable. They've been filling up with people for the past couple hundred years, there are towns, and roads, and railways, big hotels left over from when the Catskills were the place to go if you were a vacationer from the city. If you should go hiking through the wildest forests in the Catskills, places that look perfectly prehistoric, like no human has ever been there, and you wouldn't be surprised to see a woolly mammoth or a sabre-toothed tiger, you're still going to find stone walls, and the foundations of old houses. People have been all over those mountains, thick as fleas, for a long time.

And it's certain you can't find the house I lived in, not just a foundation, but a whole house with doors and windows and smoke coming out of the chimney. You can't find it on foot, and you won't see it from a helicopter, a satellite can't see it, and if you go to wherever they keep the official maps of the whole country in Washington, DC, it won't be on those maps.

What is more, if you ask any of the people in Saugerties or Palenville, or any town in and around the mountains about whether such places exist, ninety-nine out of a hundred will say they don't know what you're talking about and the hundredth one will lie to you.

You're probably familiar with the story of Rip Van Winkle. It was written in 1819 by Washington Irving, but it's pretty clear he based his story on local legends, of which there are a lot. The important part of the story is this Rip Van Winkle goes off into the mountains and meets a lot of little men, short ugly guys with beards, big heads, and

Daniel Pinkwater

little pig eyes. They're bowling and drinking homemade gin. They give Rip a few drinks, he falls asleep, and when he wakes up it's twenty years later. It's a good story, and not hard to find. You can read it for yourself.

The thing I'm working up to is this: In the impossible-to-locate place I come from the men are all short, ugly brutes with beards, big heads, and little pig eyes. I'm relieved to say that the females are nice, but the men are fairly disgusting . . . and there's bowling and drinking going on. I am not making any claims. I am just laying out the facts. You may draw your own conclusions.

2.

This hidden place in the mountains, call it a village, either didn't have a name, or it had a name and we never used it. We had a name for ourselves, "Dwerg," because that's what the old Dutch settlers called us. We called them Engels, meaning English people, which is what we call everyone who isn't us. Dwerg is a Dutch word, and Dutch people were the first non-native people who settled in the area. There are a lot of their descendants still around. Probably the Dwerg ancestors spoke Dutch way back in time. English is the language we all speak now, with some Dutch words mixed in. Some people say a Dwergish language exists, but nobody speaks it. I think dwerg means dwarf in Dutch, but also suggests gnomes or elves. Gnomes living in the forest are usually on the evil side and dangerous in stories, and apparently the local Indian tribes had stories like that, which would explain why they tried not to be in the mountains when the sun went down.

I would not describe the people in our village as evil, not at all. I would describe them as boring. Here are the options I had as a girl child growing up: help around the house, look after goats, help growing vegetables, appreciate nature. When I got to be barely almost grown up, I would be expected to marry one of the absolute slob male Dwergs. A girl would not be allowed to work in the gold mine.

Oh yes, we have a gold mine. We also have a little gold refinery, to get the metal separated from the rock and junk and impurities, and then we make it into lumpy coins. Every family has a cupboard, or closet, full of bags and bags of the stuff.

I don't have to mention that girls aren't allowed to do any of this work, which, while not necessarily all that interesting, might at least be better than goats.

We use gold, which gets swapped for money, to buy things we don't have or can't make. To do this we need someone on the outside to help us. This would be our "Englishman." You have to have an Englishman, because if some of our goofy-looking bearded Dwergs were to walk into a bank toting a bag of gold coins, it would create too much interest. Remember, I said before that one resident of a Catskill town in a hundred would lie if you asked about us? That might be just an ordinary pathological liar, or it might be our Englishman.

Being an Englishman for us Dwergs calls for complete secrecy, and it pays really well. Gold, after all. And our Englishman, Mr. Winnick, was particularly important to me, because I chose to go to school. It's a matter of choice with us Dwergs. We needed special arrangements for girls to go to school. I'm referring to regular public school, outside our weird hidden village. Quite a few girls go, the boys just about never do—education might interfere with their becoming full-bearded, boring Dwerg gold miners.

I have to explain, the Dwerg never existed who could not cover distance five times faster than an Englishman, and by Englishman I refer not to someone from England, or our clandestine agent type of Englishman, but anyone who is not a Dwerg. This includes making one's way through forests, and up and down mountains. Also, well-hidden, inaccessible, and some say magically protected, does not mean distant—our village was not so very far from a public highway—and a strong hiker could make it from our village to that public highway in maybe a little over an hour. This means that I could make it to the little shelter where we'd wait for the school bus in under fifteen minutes. This was not your usual school bus, we owned it. The driver, whose name, comically, was Mrs. Driver, either didn't know, or was sworn to pretend she didn't know anything about who we were, or where we got on from. And she would deposit us girls at the elementary school, the middle school, and the high school in Kingston, New York.

Adventures of a Dwergish Girl

Mr. Winnick had created a cover story, last names, addresses, phone numbers which if called would be answered by himself or presumably Mrs. Winnick. Not that such a phone call was ever made. Our made-up identities and details about us were just so the number of kids in the school would tally with the records. In fact it was barely noticed that we were around. Dwergs are good at being semi-invisible. My fake name was Molly O'Malley, which is a nice name, and Molly is my real name. My last name, Van Dwerg, is the same as everybody else in our village, we're all Van Dwergs. As far as the teachers and the regular kids were concerned, we were just kids from mountain-dwelling families, which exist, and are not really all that different from Dwergs. So, the facts that we were maybe a little undersized, wore old-fashioned homemade clothes, acted shy, and kept to ourselves, did not seem particularly unusual to anyone.

Most of the Dwerg kids drifted in and out of school, showing up for a couple of months or a year, and then fading away. I don't know when the Dwergs decided it was OK for girls to go outside to school, but I think it might have been a bad idea from a Dwerg point of view. Once we got an idea that goats and gold mining were not all there was, some of us, anyway one of us for certain, would get another idea.

3.

Maybe you're an expert hiker and moun-
taineer, or maybe you know one, or will
someday meet one, someone who knows the
Catskills like their own backyard, and has
been everyplace, climbed every peak, and
seen all there is to see. Ask that person if
they've ever seen a wolf. I have. You can also
ask if they've ever seen a mountain lion,
which we call catamounts. I have. I've seen
plenty of both. There would be no point in
asking if they've seen a Catskill giant, a guy
looking as rough as a male Dwerg and seven
or eight feet tall. Well, I've seen a couple of

those too. They're pretty rare. And you can ask the expert if they know anything about the Catskill witch. I'm not talking about the historical one who fought in the Revolutionary War and never missed with her musket, but an actual living witch, with powers. Almost nobody knows about her, or knows where to find her, but I do.

Here's the thing, it's a Dwerg thing, in addition to milking goats, and making cheese, and all the usual stupid things, girl-type Dwergs are expected to appreciate nature. This is not about just looking, it's about interacting. I've not only seen wolves, I've touched them—or they've touched me, brushed against me in passing, like I was a tree maybe, or another wolf. Wild deer will come right up to me to take a treat from my hand, or just to sniff me and satisfy their curiosity. And this may sound like bragging, but you do not get to see a Catskill giant if he doesn't want you to see him.

I am fairly well educated—I put in a total of a year and a half at Kingston High School. That's a lot of learning, compared to most of the Dwergs I grew up with. Also, I'm good at observing things, and thinking about what I've observed. I developed a theory that we Dwergs must be, to some degree, supernatural or magical. I mean, that's what the Native Americans thought, and the early settlers with their Rip Van Winkle stories. It's a fact that regular people can't get near wild animals the way we can, or see the things we can see that nobody else gets to see. And all the confusing us with gnomes and elves and such that the people in the towns do . . . that must be about something. Anyway, that was my theory, but try to discuss it with the grown-ups. They want to hear nothing about it, much less will they tell you anything. They want to talk about canning raspberries, or what happened today down in the mine.

My personal opinion is that Dwerg magicalness was gradually forgotten like the Dwerg language, which may or may not have existed. The Dwergs around me as I grew up were happy looking after goats and making cheese, digging up gold, and gathering together for a good old group hum.

Little by little, I came to the conclusion that I had to get away from there. I could see my friends starting to think, or not-think, like the adults, and I didn't want to lose the use of my brain. I was going to have to clear out, and live among the English people for a while, and see what the rest of the world is all about.

Of course, that meant I would be saying goodbye to my family. When I say "my family," I mean immediate, mother, father, sibling, and not the general population of the village, every one of whom is a cousin of some kind. And when I talk about how boring it is to live there, and how I wanted to leave, that is not to say that, while boring, life there is not sweet. And I love all the Dwergs. It turns out you can love persons or a place and still find them or it boring, to the point of unbearable.

My home and family, for example, could be any home and any family in the village. My mother is nice, and she is skilled at cooking, and bakes wonderful bread. She is always busy sewing and fixing, and cleaning, and doing. In the evening, after a delicious meal, maybe of vegetables and goat cheese, and hot fresh bread, we sit around the fireplace, my mother sews, my father smokes his pipe, my

younger sister, Gertie, practices to be just
like my mother. Sometimes we hum. My father starts humming, and my mother joins
in, and then we girls do. Finally, we all go to
bed. In houses all over the village families
are humming and sleeping.

In the middle of the village there is a big
outdoor oven. In the summer, the Dwerg
mothers do their baking there rather than
bake at home and make the house hot. All
year round, we gather near that oven two
or three times a week. There's no set sched-
ule, and it's at no particular time, but everyone just naturally turns up. The women
and girls stand to one side of the big oven,
and the men Dwergs to the other. We just
stand there, shifting from foot to foot. Then
someone starts humming. Soon everybody
is humming, rocking from side to side, eyes
closed. I can't say how I know this, since my
eyes are always shut, but I have always felt
certain that animals come in from the forest to watch us during these sessions. Also,
I always feel connected to the moon, and the
trees, and other planets in the solar system,
and sometimes I feel very aware of the earth

under my feet, and worms, and mosquitoes, and all kinds of unlikely things. The whole business, standing and rocking and humming, goes on for half an hour.

No one ever says anything about this business, and I don't know where it all comes from, or if it has a name, or what it's supposed to be about, or why we do it. I am pretty sure everyone feels more or less the way I do when we stop, and that is peaceful and happy.

When I thought about leaving, I was pretty sure the things I would miss most were these exercises around the community oven and my mother's bread. And I was right.

4.

Things are never really silent. You may think you're in a completely quiet place, but if you listen carefully, you'll hear a great many sounds, starting with your own breathing. You'll start to hear your heart beating, your body digesting the last meal you ate, maybe even your blood swishing in your veins. If you're in a house, the house itself makes sounds, wood expands and contracts, with noises. A fire in a fireplace, a steam radiator, a furnace, an air conditioner. People walking and talking in other rooms, or maybe other apartments, radios playing, cars and trucks in the road, insects, birds, dogs barking, the sound of the wind or rain. They all fade together and blend into the background, and you think it's quiet because you're used to those noises.

It was the same in the village. There, most of the sounds came from nature, but there were plenty of them. However, the sounds at home didn't compare to the noise in the city when some of us girl Dwergs took the bus to school. The school itself was insane with noise. It was like some kind of factory where garbage cans or church bells were made. This was just from human voices, and stamping and shuffling feet, and trucks and buses and cars on the street outside. Also there is another kind of noise that's more subtle, and gets under your skin more than all the other kinds of noise. That's the noise of people thinking. Maybe because we were Dwergs, or just because we had been raised in the comparative quiet of the woods, we'd pick up on that. It would have been unbearable, except that because there was always a bunch of us we were able to tolerate it. I can't say just why, but together we were somehow able to deflect the noise, or at least the worst effects. Maybe the more gentle and familiar Dwerg noises of our own displaced the horrid noises of the school and the city, I can't really say.

I didn't have my bunch of Dwerg girls with me on a mild summer morning when I walked out of the village, through the woods to the highway, and into the city of Kingston all by myself. The traffic on the highway made a monstrous roar, and the fumes from the engines stank and hurt my eyes. *This is going to take some getting used to*, I thought.

I walked past the high school, and into the old part of the city. There were shops and restaurants, one after another, a food market, a pawnshop. That was what I was looking for. I knew what a pawnshop was because I read about one in a story in my English class. It was on a side street, sort of dark and crummy-looking. The windows, which were not very clean, had guitars and power tools, and all kinds of junk showing. I went inside. This was the first time I had been in a shop of any kind. I was there to do business, and I didn't want to seem to be a hick kid from up in the mountains, which of course was what

I was. There was a bald-headed guy behind the counter. I walked right up, and plunked down before him a large, lumpy gold coin. "How much for this?" I asked.

His eyes bugged out. He knew what it was. I don't know if I heard him say this, or if I heard him think it, or if I just knew it from the bug-eyed expression on his face, *Dwerg-geld! It's Dwerg-geld! I've heard about this all my life, and thought it was just a story!*

"Interesting," he said, trying to sound cool. "Where did you get this, kid?"

"My father found it, or maybe it was my grandfather. It's been lying around the house for a long time," I said without lying. "Is it worth anything?"

I'd better be careful, the bald-headed guy was thinking, *little female, old-fashioned clothes, big hands and feet, she could be one herself, you don't want to mess with them— they can be dangerous.*

"Maybe a hundred bucks," he said out loud.

"My father said I shouldn't take any less than two hundred," I said. "He said anyone who offered less was trying to cheat me, and I should tell him about it."

"Didn't I say two hundred?" the bald guy said. "I'm sure that's what I said,"

"Throw in that banjo, and you've got a deal." It was an old-fashioned, long-necked banjo. It just happened to be the first thing that caught my eye, I had no particular use for it, I just didn't want Baldylocks to think he was completely getting the better of me.

I walked out of the pawnshop with the two hundred dollars and the banjo, went into another shop just up the street, and came out with a pair of blue jeans, some green sneakers, and a sweatshirt with the words St. Leon's College printed on it. I also got underwear printed with cartoons of bunnies. I looked like a regular Kingston, New York, kid. I felt pretty sophisticated.

5.

I t's not as though I sneaked out of my house in the middle of the night, stole some coins, and left my family a pathetic note. It wasn't like that at all. It was less dramatic. I told my mother that I couldn't stand living in the quaint little hidden village anymore, and wanted to give the outside world a try. She said she understood, and that when they were young she and my father had hiked into Kingston one night and gone to the movies. The picture they saw was *Gidget Goes Hawaiian*. They decided city life was not for them, and never went back. But she and my father understood, and had no objection to my trying things out for myself. They tried to get me to take a whole bag of Dwerg geld to cover expenses, but that would have been much too heavy, and I only took three coins. The whole conversation was brief and quiet and without emotion. My sister was present, but was looking out the window at some squirrels the whole time, and pretty soon my father was humming and my mother was sewing as though their daughter had not just told them she was leaving home. This, in a nutshell, is why I had to get away from the place. They are sweet, the Dwergs, and I love them of course, but I felt I owed it to my brain to skedaddle.

I walked along the street with my Dwerg clothes stuffed into my banjo case, money in the pocket of my blue jeans, and no plan of any kind. You have to understand that, for activity and distraction, compared to my little village in the mountains, being in uptown Kingston was like being in Times Square in New York City, unless you come from New York City, in which case the comparison breaks down. There were people I did not know walking on the sidewalk, there were cars going up and down the street, there were all kinds of sounds, and smells. One smell caught my attention. It was coming from a shop. Babatunji's Authentic Neapolitan Pizza it said on the sign over the door. Pizza! I'd had pizza in the high school cafeteria, but it wasn't interesting, and it didn't smell anything like this. The smell reminded me that I was hungry. I walked through the door. Inside, the smell of baking and spices was stronger and warmer, it surrounded me. There were some tables, and a counter. Behind the counter I could see the wide door of an oven. A little fat man wearing a little round hat was standing behind the counter.

"*Buongiorno!* Welcome to my pizzeria, *ragazza strana*, strange girl," he said. "How may I serve you?"

"I'm interested in having some pizza," I said. "Do you sell it by the piece, or do I have to buy a whole pie?"

"You've never had pizza before, have you?" the little fat man said.

"Practically never, and it was nothing like this is smelling."

"This is the real deal. This is the authentic pizza of Naples, Italy, my adopted home."

"Is that where you come from, Naples, Italy?"

"Well, not all that far from it."

"Such as where?"

"Sierra Leone, it's in West Africa."

"And it's close to Naples?"

"Not right next to, not very extremely close, but it's in the same hemisphere. In my heart I am a Neapolitan . . . although I have not actually been there . . . because of the pizza. *Amo la pizza*, I love pizza, and Naples is the home and the heart of pizza. My name is Arnold Babatunji, and to whom do I have the honor of serving a slice of my authentic pizza, absolutely free of charge, by way of saying hello?"

"I'm Molly O'Malley." I used my school name. I bit into my slice of pizza. "My goodness!" I said. "I happen to know something about baking, and I want to tell you, this is just wonderful!"

"So, you know something about baking," Arnold Babatunji said. "I had a feeling you might be coming for the job."

"The job?"

Arnold Babatunji pointed to sign taped to the window. The sun was shining through it, and I could read the letters backwards, Kid Helper Wanted, Inquire Within.

"It doesn't pay much, and the work isn't interesting, but you get to be around pizza. If you're anything like me, that makes it a dream job. You interested?"

I was looking past Arnold Babatunji, past the counter and the ovens. There was some kind of kitchen or prep room in the back of the store, and a back door, which was open, and beyond some garbage cans I could see a stand of trees, a little miniature forest that appealed to me very much.

6.

I always wondered if Arnold Bababtunji knew or suspected that I was a Dwerg, or maybe just that there was something irregular about me that he wasn't supposed to know. Arnold was very much a gentleman. He was careful not to ask questions that might be uncomfortable for me, things like where I lived, where I'd come from, who my parents were, or what school I went to when it wasn't summer. It didn't seem that he wasn't interested in me as a person, he was always asking what I thought about this and that, but he stayed away from anything that would have identified me. It might have been natural politeness on his part, maybe that was just how people acted in Sierra Leone, and while I had no particular reason to keep things secret, I had the natural Dwerg shyness about outsiders knowing too much. Also, whenever a regular person finds out one is a Dwerg, right away they want to know if we're the ones who handed out the drink that put Rip Van Winkle to sleep for twenty years. It gets boring.

Of course, it might also have been that Arnold wanted to be able to deny he knew my age or anything about me . . . my salary for working in the pizzeria was a dollar and a half an hour, and I was pretty sure that was below some legal minimum. Arnold said he had worked for even less when he was a kid helper in a pizzeria in Freetown, Sierra Leone, but he appreciated the chance to learn the secrets of pizza-making.

I didn't have many expenses, pizza was free, and I never got tired of it, never could and never will. And I had no rent to pay. I was fairly sure Arnold didn't know that I was living in the woods behind the pizzeria. I had found a big ball of string, and there were plenty of extra-strong giant black garbage bags in the shop. I used the string to fasten some thin saplings and branches together in a sort of arch or dome, and then I covered the dome with some of the black garbage bags, bunched the corners together and tied them to the branches, and there was my roof! I spread some garbage bags on the ground to keep the cheap fuzzy blanket I bought in a store from getting soggy, and there was my bed! There was a nice big smooth rock, just perfect for sitting on, where I could read, or attempt to play my banjo.

I had gotten a library card in the name of Molly Babatunji, giving the shop's address as my home. I didn't even know how to tune the banjo, but it was satisfying to make plaintive twanging sounds in the night. Nobody ever came near my woods. I wondered if there was something about it being a Dwerg's residence that kept it unvisited and unknown. If you looked at the little stand of trees from the back door of Arnold's shop, you wouldn't notice a thing. The black garbage bags looked like shadows behind the leaves.

My job was easy. It was sweeping and mopping, wiping tables, washing dishes, taking out the garbage, chopping wood for the oven with a little hatchet, and making up pizza boxes, which came flat, and I had to fold them. The work itself was not interesting, but being around the shop was interesting. Watching Arnold Babatunji make pizza was interesting, and talking with him was interesting. He had a lot to say, mostly all about pizza. His main interest—it would be better to call it an obsession—was classic Neapolitan pizza. I learned the sauce for this pizza has to come from either San Marzano tomatoes or Roma tomatoes, which only grow in certain parts of Italy. Arnold bought these in big cans. Also, the cheese has to come from Italian water buffalos, and the flour has to be a certain kind, the crust of a certain thickness. Arnold said he tried to come as close to the authentic thing as he could, given that he didn't have Naples water to mix the flour with.

His Neapolitan pizza was, as a matter of fact, the best thing I have ever tasted in my life, and I don't suppose that will ever change.

It is smoky, and crunchy and warm and flavorful, and . . . remember I told about those gatherings around our communal oven back in the village? Well, this pizza tastes like those sweet hum-fests feel. One day I took two pizzas, a margherita and a marinara in boxes, and walked them all the way to the hidden village, and my family's house. We warmed the pizzas up, and my mother and father and my sister, Gertie, found them "sort of interesting." but too exotic and spicy. If I didn't already think so, this would have confirmed that moving out was the right decision. I decided I'd need to have a talk with Gertie when she was older. If I could teach a Dwerg like her to appreciate and make pizza, I would have done a great thing.

Arnold's pizza culture did not stop with Naples. He made all sorts of pizzas, with various toppings, onions, peppers, sausage, things like that. Apparently every pizzeria in the United States offers those. But there are pizzas Arnold himself invented. There is the American Breakfast Pizza . . . it has cornflakes, two eggs, bacon, and a splash of orange juice and it's dusted with instant coffee powder. Then there is the Pizza da Campo, which has marshmallows, Hershey bars, and crumbled graham cracker. The Pizza Africana has bananas . . . Arnold explained to me that there is a whole banana culture in Africa that we Americans know nothing about, lots of varieties very different from the big yellow ones we eat. The Pizza Elvis has those, plus peanut butter. Arnold also invented the Pizza Ebraica, which has slices of gefilte fish, which is a kind of ground-up fish log that comes in jars.

I, personally, stick with the Neapolitan style, and will do so for the rest of my life. Arnold says that New York City pizza can be a close second to Naples. As a Dwerg-American, this makes me proud.

7.

I'm sure Arnold Babatunji could never understand why I wouldn't want to spend the rest of my life becoming a pizza chef. He had already said that if I was still with him after two years he would begin letting me help make the dough. He had been a pizza apprentice in Freetown, and he expected to pass on the things he had learned, and I hope he will. I was not the first kid helper to work for him, and I knew I would not be the last, starting when it got too cold to sleep in the trees out back of the shop. Still, it was interesting working in the pizzeria. Not the work, the work was the complete opposite of interesting, but being around the shop, observing and listening to the customers who came in held my attention day after day.

Babatunji's Authentic Neapolitan Pizza was located just a few feet outside the old stockade. A stockade is a kind of log fence, a fortification. Think of those forts they always show in Western movies, that's what a stockade is like. Of course the actual stockade, made of logs, is long gone, but people know where it used to be. It took in about eight blocks, roughly thirty-two acres, and the Dutch settlers had built it in 1658, to keep the Indians out.

The town was called Wiltwyck then. It got to be Kingston when the Dutch handed it over to the English, who later burned the whole place down in 1777 as a hotbed of patriots during the American Revolution. The Dutch people lived in the town, and the Native Americans lived outside. They all farmed the soil, and grazed their animals in roughly the same area. Every now and then a bunch of Dutch types would drink some gin and go find some Indians and bop them on the head. Similarly, some Indians would drink some gin and go find some Dutch folks and bop them on the head. On some occasions, both the Indians and the Dutch would drink some gin, get the same idea, and go looking for each other. Apparently, in between these outbursts, they all got along reasonably well, trading with one another and so forth.

So, in 1658, Peter Stuyvesant, who was the governor of New York, ordered the settlers to build a wall, and they did so. They then built some neat stone houses, and built them quite well. The proof of this is that the stone walls withstood the burning by the British, the houses were restored in the space of a year, and some of them are still standing today. The city grew over the centuries, and spread out, but the stockade area, or where the stockade had been, sort of remained the center. It had the courthouse, and there were shops and offices, and houses built in the 17th, 18th, 19th, and 20th centuries, all in this fairly small and compact space. Plus there's a big church, with a graveyard where everybody is buried, and there are people living in some of the old houses whose families go back all the way to when the place was called Wiltwyck. It all fits together, and I liked walking around the neighborhood. It was like walking in and out of time and history.

The people who came into Arnold Babatunji's pizzeria were as much of a mix as the old Stockade District itself. All different sorts of people, that's what I liked best about living away from the Dwerg village, where everybody was . . . well, a Dwerg.

8.

Dwergs don't need much sleep, or anyway, this Dwerg. A couple of hours wrapped up in my fuzzy blanket under my garbage bag roof, or maybe sleeping up in the branches of a tree, and I'd need to get up and walk around. So I was on the streets of the old stockade at all hours of the night, which was how I came to know that the place was overrun with ghosts. It stands to reason, the area had been there for such a long time, there were houses that had been continuously occupied for multiple generations, and the graveyard was just packed. Add to this

Native American ghosts whose families had been in the neighborhood for nobody knows how long. Not everybody who's dead goes in for ghosting, I'm not sure how it works, but certain ones do, and they tend to come out at night. The old streets were crowded with departed when it got dark. I can't imagine how a neighborhood could be any ghostier.

Although, as a Dwerg, I may tend to be a little shy with live people, I feel very comfortable with the dead. Not everybody can see ghosts, and those who can may not be able to see all the ghosts there are. I can see them all, and if you are polite to them, they will be polite to you. I developed nodding acquaintances, hello and how do you do, with many nightwalkers, and I had some warm friendships with ghostly dogs and cats. Yes, there are pet ghosts, dog and cat ones, and mouse ghosts too, what did you suppose?

9.

I had a favorite ghost, Roger Van Tussen-vuxel. He appeared to be about sixteen years old, with freckles and reddish curly hair. He always wore blue jeans, blown-out at the knees, and a T-shirt with the words Rock 'n' Roll Is Here to Stay printed on it. He spoke like an ordinary Kingston kid, with maybe the odd Dutch word mixed in. I was surprised to learn he was born in 1750. I usually ran into Roger during my nightly walks on a street called Frog Alley where there's an old ruined house surviving from the 1600s.

"You're always hanging out around here," I said to Roger Van Tussenvuxel. "Is this the place you haunt? Did you die here or something?"

"You've probably heard about these ghosts who appear on the stairs every night at precisely 11:20 P.M. and moan or rattle chains or something," Roger said. "This happens, but it's really rare. I don't know a single ghost who carries on like that. I don't mean to cast shade on any of my fellow shades, but I think that kind of behavior is sort of neurotic. You know, there are people who can be perfectly nice, and even lovable, but at the same time they will be a pain in the *zitvlak?*"

"You're talking about everybody I used to live with."

"Well, those are the types who go in for haunting. Most ghosts are not like that. The ones you see around here doing the spook walk have just come up for a nice tour around the old neighborhood."

"Come up from where?"

"From the underworld. Surely you've heard of it."

"Not really, assuming you do not refer to gangsters and such."

"No, I mean the underworld that's been around forever, and mentioned in Greek mythology and everyplace else, and not many living people have had a look at it, so it is generally completely misunderstood."

"Never heard of it."

"That surprises me, you being a Dwerg and all, and pretty much supernatural around the edges your own self."

"You know about Dwergs, and can tell I'm one?"

"Listen, when you've been dead as long as I have, you pick up all kinds of stuff."

Roger Van Tussenvuxel was sort of cute, I have to say. He had nice blue eyes. I didn't have a crush on him, what with his being dead and all, and I am just mentioning. He knew a lot about history, especially the history of Wiltwyck, New York, later called Kingston, and especially from about 1760 to the present. He told me I was his favorite semi-supernatural living person, which I considered a compliment, even though I knew all his other friends were ghosts.

It was my practice to sit down with a slice of pizza and a cold root beer at one of the tables on one of my breaks at the pizzeria. Arnold Babatunji told me I could have as many breaks as I wanted. I usually wanted five or six. On these breaks, while waiting for my slice to cool, I would enjoy looking over any customers who were on hand. The variety of customers was always entertaining, fat and thin, fit and sloppy, tall and short, rich and poor, different sexes, different colors, and besides being interesting in the ways they looked, it was fun to see what kind of pizza each one would order, and how they'd eat it, one-handed and folded, New York City style, or knife and fork, or waving it in the air like a flag and snapping at the flopping tip of the slice. Also it was fun listening to them, noting how they talked, and what they talked about.

What I was not prepared to see was my friend Roger Van Tussenvuxel, in broad daylight, sitting at the table across from me.

"Roger! What are you doing here?"

"Came for pizza. Would you be willing to pass me your slice of pizza?"

"You eat pizza? I thought ghosts are insubstantial, have no physical bodies, and are unable to so much as lift a slice of pizza, let alone eat it."

"This is true, but we can sniff things. Just let me inhale over your slice, I won't do it any harm."

"Also, how come you're out in daylight?"

"There's no rule against it. Ghosts prefer the dark for a variety of reasons."

"Such as not upsetting living people? What would the customers here think if they knew you were a walking, talking, sniffing deadster?"

"I doubt they can see me. Takes a special kind of person. As close as even an unusually sensitive type is likely to come would be to see me as a sort of thick place in the air, or an almost-shadow, if that makes any sense."

"I can see you fine, better than at night."

"You're a Dwerg."

"Would you like to take a whiff of a slice with pepperoni?"

"Oh, yes, please!"

10.

Ihad no idea whether Roger Van Tussen-vuxel had done anything noteworthy or interesting when he was alive. He may have. He may have fought in the Revolution, but he never said anything about it. Maybe he was on the British side in the Revolution and that was why he didn't want to talk about his life, or maybe he was just modest. Mostly he concentrated on looking and acting like a contemporary teenager, talking about rock 'n' roll music, and sports teams, even though he was born in 1750.

I did get to see, and even had "Good evening" said to me, by a ghost who had been really important in life. This was a tall black woman. She wasn't just tall, she was powerful, you could see from the way she moved, smooth, gliding, like some kind of queen. She wore big full skirts, with an apron over them that went down to the ground, and a sort of turban or cap, and little squinty gold eyeglasses with big calm eyes behind them. She wasn't there every night, just once in a while, and all the ghosts got excited when she turned up.

I asked around, and learned this was the ghost of Sojourner Truth. I got a book from the Kingston Public Library that told all about her.

Sojourner Truth had been born a slave near Kingston in 1797. That's right, there were slaves in the North. Slavery in New York didn't end until 1827 and then it was by drips and drops. Sojourner Truth went to the courthouse right there in the Stockade District and sued to recover her son, who had been illegally sold into a state that still had slavery, and she won her case. A black woman had never done such a thing before. She traveled all over the country speaking against slavery, and after the Civil War she spoke for human rights and women's rights. She died in 1883, so she must have seen electric light, possibly used the telephone, and might even have taken a ride in an automobile, all those things had come about within eighteen years of the last time a person could own another person in the United States. The ghosts respected her a lot for the role she played, and so did I.

11.

It occurred to me that, with the exception of Arnold Babatunji, and a couple of customers who came into the shop and with whom I would exchange a word or two, I was associating exclusively with the dead. This is not to say that the ghosts of uptown Kingston were not very nice, much as the Dwergs in my village were also nice, but I had to admit I was not finding what I had left home to find . . . whatever that may have been.

I was just thinking these thoughts while taking a break at the pizzeria, when a girl I had never seen before sat down at my table. She had two slices and a Dr Pepper, was approximately my age, and had a nice face, and beautiful straight black hair.

"You look completely normal," the girl said. "What happened to the *Little House on the Prairie* outfit you and your friends used to wear?"

"I beg your pardon?"

"You and a bunch of other kids, friends of yours, I assume. You all had the long skirts, and the big shoes, and went around in a flock, not talking to anybody."

"Oh, you mean in high school!"

"Right. I almost didn't recognize you in normal clothes. My name is Leni Toomay." She stuck her hand out.

I shook hands with her. "Molly O'Malley," I said. It's possible to meet someone and know right away that you have something in common, and you want to be friends. It was like that with Leni. I felt like I already knew her.

"So what is it, do you and those others all belong to some kind of old-fashioned church up in the hills, and it's real strict and makes you wear the old-fashioned clothes and not talk to modern people?"

"Well, not quite, but sort of," I said. I think I've mentioned that I didn't feel I was supposed to keep being a Dwerg a big secret, but at the same time it didn't seem like a good idea to go around announcing it. I didn't feel it would do any harm if I told Leni, and then she said something that surprised me a little.

"Know what we used to call you and your friends? The Dwergs."

"Really."

"Don't be offended. It was perfectly good-humored, and not racist or anything, because as you know, Dwergs don't really exist."

"Is that a fact?"

"Well, I don't know, maybe they used to exist and now they're extinct, or blended into the general population. My own ancestors included the local Native American tribe, and they both blended in and got pushed out to reservations in the West. If I thought calling you girls Dwergs was mean-spirited, I would never have stood for it."

"No, it's OK. I can see how we would have looked like Dwergs to you."

"As a matter of fact, there may be proof that Dwergs did exist at some point. My aunt's boyfriend, Angus, runs the pawnshop, and a kid came in with what he thinks is a Dwerg coin, must be really old. I've seen it."

"What did it look like?"

"It was sort of lumpy, and heavy, and made of gold. Had what might have been the image of a goat on one side, and what looked like a wedge of cheese on the other."

I dug one of my coins out of my pocket and put it on the table. "Anything like this?"

Leni looked at the coin, then she looked at me. I found her expression very entertaining, and I had fun watching her run the various possibilities through her mind.

"Keep this under your hat," I said.

"So . . . so . . . I mean . . . you . . . and they . . . and . . ."

"Yep."

"Wow."

"Your pizza's getting cold."

"Wow."

12.

Leni and I were walking down Broadway, toward the Rondout Creek, which connects with the Hudson River. It was another old part of town, but not nearly as old as uptown. The Rondout is a pretty big creek, and there are old boatyards that could handle fair-sized rivercraft. Along the way there are all kinds of buildings from the first half of the twentieth century, I supposed, and shops and stores, a place that sold fish, and a couple of the many hot dog stands that are a feature of Kingston. I have to give a tip to tourists and travelers about Kingston hot dogs. It is this: Don't. Consider, I had more or less just come out of the woods, and had never seen or heard of, let alone tasted, a hot dog in my entire life, and yet I was able to tell that the standard hot dog in Kingston was a pathetic imitation of something real, and would depress a moose. They're pink, they're the exact same hot dogs you can buy in any supermarket, the cheapest kind, same goes for the buns, low-grade yellow mustard, and if you ask for chili on your dog, you get watery horrible stuff that is an insult to the chili-eating world and all persons of good will.

Leni explained that the street dog in New York City, while a danger to one's health, at least tastes good, and the ones sold at papaya juice stands, and also at Coney Island, are cultural treasures and worth a trip from anywhere.

"What are we waiting for? Let's go there now," I said.

"That's a topic for another conversation I'm looking forward to having," Leni said. "For now, there's something I want to show you."

"And what would that be?"

"Wait and see. We're almost there."

Leni and I had been hanging out almost any time I wasn't working, and sometimes she would visit the pizzeria during my work hours and keep me company. Arnold Babatunji already knew her before I met her, and he liked her.

We made our way along the bank of the creek. "General Vaughn and his troops came along this route the opposite way we're going in 1777, when they burned the whole town of Kingston," Leni said.

"I read about it," I said. "Has that got anything to do with what you want to show me?"

"We have arrived at what I want to show you," Leni said. "Are you good at climbing?"

"I sleep in a tree."

"So a chain-link fence eight feet high won't be a problem. And here it is, and over we go."

A few feet beyond the fence was the entrance to some sort of cave, great big open arches. "What is this?" I asked.

"Cave."

"I can see that. What cave? What sort of cave?"

"It's the Kingston Cave, goes on and on, under the whole eastern part of the city. It goes down and down too. It's not so much a cave as a mine. They used to dig limestone to make cement out of here. Apparently it was just the right kind of limestone, because they dug out a lot of it. The mine goes on for thousands and thousands of feet, there are columns, and a couple of big underground lakes. Also, it's got all kinds of cave things happening, stalagmites, and huge columns of ice, it gets cavier and cavier all the time. In a few hundred years people won't be able to tell it's not a natural cavern. You feel like exploring a little? I brought a flashlight."

"Let's go, and do not worry about what could happen should you use up your batteries. I can see in the dark like a bat."

"Is that a Dwerg thing?"

"I suppose so. And I've been in a cave before, only just a little one."

The cave was great. Starting out there were great big chambers. You could see trucks had been driven in and out. There were massive columns holding up the roof. Then we came upon long tunnels that went left and right, and always downward. We passed old rusty mining machinery, and cars from the 1920s and 1930s. It was cold and there were bats. We almost stepped into a huge black lake, and I could hear fish jumping and splashing.

"This is a fantastic cave," I told Leni.

"I knew you'd like it."

We explored the cave for about an hour going in, and maybe an hour and a half getting out, because it was uphill, and we got a little bit lost for a while.

"We should come back with at least four flashlights, extra batteries, and some lunch," I said. "I want to find out how far this thing goes."

"There are supposed to be ghosts," Leni said. "I forgot to mention."

"Ghosts a problem for you?"

"Nah, I like them."

"Good. So do I."

13.

"Roger Van Tussenvuxel! I've been looking for you!"

"And you found me."

"There's something I wanted to ask you about."

"Ask away."

"Late the other night, I was taking a walk around the neighborhood."

"As one does."

"Right. And I saw a bunch of redcoats."

"Redcoats, as in . . ."

"As in British soldiers from the time of

the Revolutionary War. I never saw them before, and I thought I'd ask you."

"This is a mistake people keep making. You think because I'm a ghost I know every other ghost. It's annoying. Imagine if I assumed because you're a Dwerg that you knew every other Dwerg there was."

"I do."

"Well, it's not a good example, then. Anyway, I don't know these British soldier ghosts, never saw them in my death, besides which, it's a little surprising they're around here."

"Why is that?"

"Well, I don't know if British soldiers died around here in any numbers, or even at all. The story is they marched in, set fire to the place, and marched out. I never heard about any of them making the supreme sacrifice."

"Something about them puzzled me. Some of them were eating hot dogs."

"To that I say 'Ick,'" Roger Van Tussenvuxel said. "If they got them around here."

"And you told me ghosts do not eat."

"This is true. Possibly what you saw were the ghosts of hot dogs."

"Ghostly food? Is that a thing?"

"How do I know? Am I Professor Knows Everything or someone? But if they were eating hot dogs, I suggest what you saw was not ghostly."

"You mean they were other than ghosts?"

"Other."

"Then what?"

"Again she assumes I have the answers."

14.

There's a little brick building on Fair Street, near the Old Dutch Church, that's maybe a hundred and fifty years old. At the street level is a shop, Cows and Frogs, a gift shop, I suppose you'd call it. It sells little ceramic cows and little ceramic frogs, pictures of cows, pictures of frogs, dish towels embroidered with . . . you guessed it. Cow greeting cards, and also frog ones. I guess it could be the favorite store of people who like cows, or frogs, or cows and frogs. It belongs to Isabel Backus, and she and

her husband Billy Backus live in an apartment on the upper floor of the building. This
upper floor, in addition to the Backuses'
apartment, has the studio of WKIN, a radio station. It's a one-man operation, Billy
Backus is the owner, the engineer, the announcer, the disc jockey, the news reader,
and also the janitor and the guy who sells
advertising spots. When he has to run an
errand for Isabel Backus, or when it's time
for lunch, or he needs to take a nap, he just
shuts the radio station down. Billy Backus
is also Professor Knows Everything, and
has a program every day called *Ask the Professor*, on which he answers questions that
people phone in. He's a genius, and always
knows the answers.

I know about Professor Knows Everything because Arnold Babatunji has WKIN
playing on the radio in his pizzeria all the
time. He says that he learned English by
listening to the radio, and also, if you listen to Billy Backus enough, it is the same
as getting a university education. Billy
Backus was the smartest child ever born
in Kingston, and had the highest IQ ever

recorded. Before he was five he could speak nine languages, had written a book about astronomy, could play the piano and the xylophone, and gave a concert at Carnegie Hall in New York City in which he played both instruments at once. When he was eleven he was a full professor at the State University in Albany, New York. He taught ancient history, Greek, Latin, and Home Economics. Then he got tired of the whole business of being a boy genius, and he got a job cleaning out furnaces. Later, he married Isabel, bought the little brick building, and took over the radio station, which was already in it. Isabel, as I mentioned earlier, was interested in frogs and cows.

Typical questions on *Ask the Professor* might go something like this: A listener calls in and asks, "How do you make *krupnik?*" and Billy Backus says, "*Krupnik* is a thick Polish soup, with a base of vegetable or meat broth, and it has potatoes and barley groats. *Krupnik* can also contain *wloszczyzna*, a combination of diced vegetables, and also meat, onions, and mushrooms." Another caller might ask, "How high is up?"—to which the professor could reply, "If something is high up, it is a long way above the ground, or sea level, or possibly you." Some of the questions are meant to stump or confuse Billy, such as, "What do you sit on, sleep on, and use to brush your teeth?" The answer he gave to that one was, "A chair, a bed, and a toothbrush."

Besides answering questions from the audience, Billy Backus sometimes gives a little lecture or history lesson, or explains something at length. On one particular day during the time I was living under and in the trees behind Arnold Babatunji's pizzeria, the topic was famous gangsters who had visited or lived in Kingston. I found this program fascinating, and as it turned out, useful.

"Today, Professor Knows Everything will tell you of the blood-stained, bullet-riddled, and bathtub gin—drenched days of our fair city's gangster past. Yes, Kingston had more than its fair share of malefactors, evildoers, thugs, bullyboys, and cardsharpers. I will tell you tales of violence and horror, but first . . . Our program is brought to you through the courtesy of the good people at Lonesome Cowboy Hot Wieners . . . five locations in

Adventures of a Dwergish Girl

Kingston . . . Remember friends, it's one dollar for two dogs and a cup of generic cola . . . Ask for yours with chili, or *wloszczyzna* . . . yumm.

"Now back to tales of the Roaring Twenties and the Gasping Thirties, when men in hats traded potshots and machine-gun bursts on the historic streets of old Kingston. First, it's easy to see why the criminal element found a home here. They were all New Yorkers, from Manhattan, and Albanians, from Albany, and the Catskills and Kingston are in between those cities. These were the days before air-conditioning, when anybody who could afford it would head this way in the summer to breathe, and also eat blueberries. So they knew how to get here. And besides climate, lovely scenery, and fresh produce, the neighborhood has lakes and ponds, and especially the beautiful Ashokan Reservoir, from which New York City gets its water, all ideal for sinking the remains of business competitors.

"And of course, our local police department, while second to none, simply didn't have resources to deal with large numbers of heavily armed, experienced meanies.

"Old timers can still remember some of the more colorful criminals, such as Legs Rhinestone, a stone-hearted killer with the most beautiful limbs in the underworld, Jilly Two-vests, cold-blooded, and hot-headed, he was feared by friends and enemies alike. Also seen on our streets were Freddie the Frog, Daffy the Duck, and Goofy the Schnook, the aristocrats of crime."

Every afternoon at one, Billy Backus would do a short commercial for Babatunji's Authentic Neapolitan Pizza before closing down the radio station for lunch. He would then appear at our pizzeria. Arnold Babatunji would have the professor's pizza ready, pepperoni with olives. Of course, Arnold did not charge for the pizza, and Billy Backus did not charge for the radio commercial. He said this is what is called a quid pro quo.

I would be the one to serve the former boy genius his pizza, and also an ice-cold bottle of Dr. Pedwee's Grape Soda, a popular health beverage made with mostly natural grapes.

"I enjoyed the program about the old-time gangsters, Professor Knows Everything," I said.

"Call me Billy."

"Thanks, Billy, I will. Anyway, I thought it was interesting, the tough guys way back in history."

"There are still a few around, beside the ghost of Legs Rhinestone," Billy said.

"Gangsters, or ghosts?"

"Both. Ghosts and gangsters, and at least one gangster ghost."

"So you know about the ghost activity here in the neighborhood . . . What am I saying? Of course you know about it. You know about everything."

"So it is said. You know the old saying, 'Once a boy genius, always a boy genius.'"

"No, I never heard that one."

"Well, it's an old saying, and yes, I know about the nightly spook walk, and I know you wander around late at night, and visit with the honored former citizens of the town. Dwergs tend to be active at odd hours."

"You know I'm a Dwerg."

"Well, obviously."

"So, let me ask you this, would there be any reason for a lot of ghostly British troops, or maybe they're Hessian mercenaries, anyway redcoats of the Revolutionary period, to show up on the streets around here?"

"You're talking about that crowd that was on Frog Alley the other night, gnawing on frankfurters. They're not ghosts."

"Not? They're alive?"

"I didn't say that, just that they aren't ghosts."

"If they're not ghosts, and thus not dead, they're alive, aren't they? What other categories exist?"

"You'd be surprised."

"So what are they, these soldiers?"

"Don't let this get around, but that is something I do not know."

15.

Leni Toomay and I were sitting on a low wall, drinking bottles of Dr. Pedwee's Grape. "You know, the common belief is that Dwergs have huge hoards of gold," she said. "But people say that sort of thing about any group they know nothing about, not to mention groups they think are nonexistent. I hope you won't think I listen to rumors or anything like that, but I have to ask you. Are you rich? I mean with money, I know that kind of story gets exaggerated."

"No, it's true, we have tons of the stuff. Why do you ask?"

"Bus tickets to New York City and back would come to about ninety bucks, and then there's the papaya juice and at least a couple of hot dogs, which are completely different from what you might think. Is that something you can handle?"

"Apart from the fact that I have access to more or less unlimited quantities of gold, I have no rent to pay, get my meals for nothing, and hardly buy anything, so even though Arnold Babatunji pays me a disgraceful wage, I could afford it even if I wasn't a Dwerg zillionaire. When do you want to go?"

"Understand, if I had any money I'd be happy to kick in my share, but I don't. However I will make myself useful by guiding you around the city, and also I have some information to impart that you will find interesting."

"You think I will need a guide in New York City? I had no problem adjusting to Kingston, and as a Dwerg, I can navigate the whole of the Catskill Mountains, no trouble at all."

"As a Native American, I have inherited

woodland skills that may be the match for yours, but the Apple is a little different?"

"The Apple? What's that?"

"The Big Apple; Gotham; the City That Never Sleeps; New York, New York; the City So Nice They Named It Twice."

"So you know your way around."

"I modestly say yes."

"Been down there a lot?"

"This will be my third trip."

16.

The bus terminal was just past the diner. I asked Leni about it as we passed. "What goes on in there? You ever been inside?"

"You've never been in the diner?"

"I wouldn't be asking if I had."

"It's a diner. Lots of items on the menu. All diners are good for breakfasts, eggs cooked several ways, and diner home fries are good, but the special thing is the tapioca pudding. They do it right."

"I've never had it."

"So, you more or less survive exclusively on Babatunji's pizza?"

"There's no more or less about it. I live on Babatunji's pizza, and nothing else. So does Babatunji."

"Not what I'd call a balanced diet."

"It's plenty balanced. I get something from the wheat group, something from the sauce group, and something from the cheese group every day. Plus occasionally something from the pepperoni group. Babatunji says it's nature's most perfect food."

"I'll be interested to hear what you have to say after you have some papaya juice."

"The object of our trip to the city."

"One of the objects. And here's our bus."

The only bus I had been on was the school bus that used to pick up Dwerg girls and take us to Kingston. This bus was a lot bigger, and fancier. The outside was shiny metal, and there were big, comfy seats inside. It was slightly dark, the windows were tinted like sunglasses, the interior of the bus smelled of air-conditioned air, and we could feel a cool rush coming out of little vents and nozzles.

We settled into seats, the doors closed with a whoosh and a clunk, and the bus moved forward, smooth and silent. I liked it. It was worth twenty-two dollars and fifty cents just to ride in the thing, much less be taken to New York City.

There were just a few passengers on the bus. People got on and off at various towns we stopped at on the way. It was fun looking out the window, and as we rode, we talked.

"I want you to know that I have never breathed a word to anyone about you being a Dwerg," Leni said.

"I wouldn't mind if you had," I said. "Not that I mean to advertise it, but at the same time, it's not some big dark secret."

"Just the same, you're a friend of mine, and it should be up to you whether you want anybody to know you're Dwergish. I just wouldn't want you to think it was me spreading private stuff around."

"OK, I get it," I said. "You have not outed me as a Dwerg, which anybody who knew anything about anything would have guessed just looking at me." Even though Dwerg means dwarf, very few Dwergs would qualify as one, still we are on the diminutive side, definitely shorter than average, and only a bit taller than an official dwarf. Add to this, we tend to have hands and feet just a little big for our height, and it is said we have a kind of look in our eyes that other folks don't have. What I'm getting at is, if you know what a Dwerg looks like, then you'll know when you're looking at one.

Of course, very few people know what a Dwerg looks like. The only live person to know for sure that I was one was Billy Backus, who knows everything, and is a professor of knowing everything. I thought of him as a nice guy with good manners, and I doubted he was who Leni was leading up to telling me about.

"You know, you're not the only one who talks to the ghosts around here. And they're all such gossips. I'm pretty sure it was one of them who gave you away."

"Gave me away to whom, and what difference does it make?"

"Well, my aunt's boyfriend is Angus Mc-Melvin, who runs the pawnshop."

"We've met."

"Well, he suspects you."

"Suspects me of what?"

"Suspects you of being a Dwerg."

"That's hardly surprising when you consider I cashed in a Dwerg coin at his shop. I have to ask you, so what?"

"So, he has unsavory friends."

"Something else that doesn't surprise me. He looks to be a pretty unsavory friend himself."

"Well some of his unsavory friends are gangsters."

"And he told them about the gold coin."

"Told and showed it to them."

"And being gangsters, they got all interested."

"Yes."

"Who exactly are these gangsters?"

"Well the worst one is Leg Rhinestone."

"Isn't that *Legs* Rhinestone?"

"It used to be Legs. Now it's Leg. The other one's wooden."

"He lost one."

"He led a dangerous life."

"Which leads us to a point I was about to make. I believe he's dead, is he not?"

"Well, yes."

"So, a ghost."

"Of course."

"So, what does he want to do, sniff my remaining gold coins? I don't see that this is a big deal."

"I just wanted to make you aware."

"I am aware."

17.

Leni told me that the Port Authority Bus Terminal in Manhattan is officially designated as one of the ten ugliest buildings in the world, which I find easy to believe. It is huge, covers as much area as the whole Stockade District in uptown Kingston, and has 190,000 people moving through it every day. About six thousand bus trips begin and end there, and there are connections to various subways, local buses in Manhattan, and taxicabs, lined up outside the building waiting for fares. I would say the atmosphere in the terminal, which New Yorkers call the Port of New York Authority, or PONY, or the Port of Authority, is about fifty percent air and the rest diesel fumes, the smells of 190,000 people, and behind it all what Leni said was the signature aroma of New York City, urine and frying onions. The onion fragrance comes from various stands where sausage and peppers are prepared. I'm not even curious as to where the other smell comes from. Another statistic, it takes about three minutes for a Dwerg to lose her mind in this building. "Get me out of here!" I said to Leni. I more or less screamed it, and I was digging my fingers into her arm.

"See? I told you that you needed an experienced guide," she said, and guided me to a moving staircase that took us down to the street, and outside. The outside was very much like the inside, only it had daylight and slightly more oxygen, but also more fumes from cars and buses.

"So this is hell," I said.

"No, this is Manhattan. Hell is in Brooklyn. Now we are going to walk across town, it's not very far, and then we will hang a left, and walk forty-four blocks north to 86th Street. There we will find Papaya King, where we will be refreshed, and then as a special treat, we will take the subway back to Midtown, which is where we are now."

Walking on 42nd Street was complicated, there was an astonishing number of people, all walking fast, and not colliding with one another. It was a bit stressful, but not life- and sanity-threatening like the bus terminal. Leni was fairly good at navigating among the other pedestrians, and I was picking up skills quickly. I soon even had time to take in some features of the street—displays, most of them pretty vulgar, outside movie theaters, shops with window displays, a smell of hot nuts coming from one shop, and of chocolate from another. I was also becoming able to view the various New Yorkers, who come in a vast range of shapes, colors, and sizes.

I have mentioned that, as a Dwerg, I am a fantastic walker. I don't know if her Native American background had anything to do with it, but Leni was very good for a normal human. It is not that we were hurrying, or trying to put on speed, but we kept up a brisk pace, skirting obstacles, timing our gait so we'd arrive at cross streets as the traffic lights turned green, observing people and things, and enjoying a conversation as we covered the forty-four blocks to 86th Street. I was getting to like walking in New York City.

I was getting to like New York City itself. The buildings, big and small, had different textures and characteristics, the shop window displays were interesting, and the other people on the street were moving along in much the same way we were. It was like a big, blocks-long dance, with everybody weaving in and out, joining in the procession and dropping out of it, turning in from corners, and turning out, and everybody with their own style, their own individual costumes and activities, some traveling in couples or groups, some with a child, some of them children on their own, some with a pet, some sauntering, some hurrying, and all to the background of noises from cars, buses, trucks, people talking and hollering, garbage cans being shifted, buildings under construction or being torn down, which goes on constantly, and the rumble of the subway under our feet. People didn't make eye contact much, or speak or nod to each other. It must have looked like they were cold and distant, but I got the sense that they actually felt friendly to one another. I felt friendly to them. It wasn't really so different from uptown Kingston, or the Dwerg village. We were all exercising the same skills, each in their own personal and different way. The answer came to me to the questions that must occur to every single person on first coming to Manhattan, "How can anybody live here? Why do they want to live here?"

The answer New Yorkers would give is, "Because we can."

We had been in motion since we got off the bus three-quarters of an hour earlier. When we finally came to a stop, it was when we had arrived at Papaya King. It was a stand, similar to several hot dog stands we had walked past. This one had a lot of signs and slogans all over: Tropical Deliciousness and Snappy Frankfurters, one said. Hot Dogs Tastier Than Filet Mignon, was another. Nature's Own Revitalizer, and Vitamin Packed, Health Giving. The stand was on the corner of 86th Street and Third Avenue. It had a window, open to the street, at the 86th Street end, where you could walk up, order something, and take it away. Around the corner, it was all glass, with a narrow metal counter facing the windows. The space where customers could stand was comparatively small, most of the space was behind the counter.

The place was crowded with people holding big paper cups of juice, and gobbling hot dogs on buns, dripping sauerkraut and mustard. In what I was coming to understand was a New York style, they were able to manage in a small space without getting mustard and sauerkraut all over themselves. Leni told me that a New Yorker can eat a large slice of pizza, and read the newspaper, while running to catch a bus, not get run over and killed, and show up at work without pizza stains or hunks of cheese on clothing.

There was a bunch of guys working behind the counter. They moved fast. Leni shouted our order to them, and I paid. It was two hot dogs, mustard and kraut, and a large papaya juice apiece.

I had never had filet mignon, and didn't know what it was, but I was sure the hot dogs were tastier than it could possibly be. I was impressed, but the real surprise, the real reason to ride the bus for three hours, and walk fifty blocks, was the papaya juice. Here's how I would describe the papaya juice . . . I can't describe the papaya juice, it's smooth and soft and creamy, I can tell you that. I can't tell you exactly what it tastes like. It's papaya, a taste all its own, and it has some kind of power. You can feel it working on your whole body, and especially your brain, from the first sip. The stuff is jumping with vitamins, and all the signs around Papaya King don't do it justice. My first thought was that I had to tell Arnold Babatunji about this. I respected him, and knew he would not be distressed to learn there was something at least the equal of his pizza. If it were possible to have both things together, that could be the start of a new religion.

"Can we take some of this back to Kingston?" I asked Leni.

"We can, but it won't be like this. It doesn't travel well. You have to have it straight from the secret, patent-protected, papaya-juice juicing machine. So, what do you think of it?"

"I'm emotional. I would burst into tears, only the stuff has me feeling too happy to cry."

"See? That's what I admire about you. You appreciate stuff. The average New Yorker stops in and drinks this stuff, and naturally loves it, but doesn't realize there would be no perfectly good reason for this whole city to exist, except you can get papaya juice here."

"Where do papayas come from?"

"Southern part of this hemisphere, also from the produce section of most supermarkets."

"Do you think the Papaya King would sell me a secret, patent-protected, papaya-juice juicing machine? I want to give one to Arnold Babatunji."

"It's a closely guarded secret."

"I'm prepared to pay any price."

"Then, yes."

18.

Most subway entrances in New York are straightforward sets of stairs going down, surrounded by iron railings that look to be about a hundred years old, and probably are. But some subway entrances are inside big buildings, or partially inside them. The stairs might be set back from the sidewalk in a big open space. And most of the subway stations are just what you'd expect, a set of railroad tracks with a platform running alongside, but there are big stations that are like an underground plaza, with booths where you can buy subway tokens and passes, shops of various kinds, maybe a barber shop, maybe a food shop, a pizzeria, a hot dog stand. The idea of getting something to eat in the subway, which is filthy and foul-smelling, struck me as insane, but I suppose if you are a New Yorker in a hurry, and do not care if you live or die, or perhaps do not believe in the germ theory, it's something you might do.

The entrance to the subway near Papaya King is one of those partially-in-a-building ones, and partway down the stairs is the entrance to a shop, not underground and not above ground, with a strange assortment of goods in the windows. On our walk uptown, I had noticed that most of the shop windows showed carefully arranged and artistic displays, mostly of expensive-looking merchandise. This half-underground place had an assortment that could only be described as crazy, a plastic model spaceship, taxidermied squirrels, plates, cups, and saucers with a crummy image of the Statue of Liberty, T-shirts with a picture of King Kong, and a set of bagpipes. In gold letters on the window were the words Das Kleine Museum. Maybe the papaya in our bloodstreams was making us seek experiences and adventure. Leni and I drifted through the door.

If the window had been crazy, the inside of the shop was a complete insane asylum. There were model airplanes, and inflated cartoon animals hanging on wires from the ceiling, shelves and display cases had plastic dinosaurs, carved wooden masks that sort of looked like they were real tribal masks, but you could see they weren't. Rusty spears, swords, and pool cues leaned in a corner, there were books about flying saucers, and vegetarian cooking, racks with weird articles of clothing, sweaters with nuts and shells worked into the knitting; hats with logos saying NY Mets, Yankees, Yorkville; and a big dollhouse, complete with electric lights and tiny furnishings.

The proprietor was a tall guy with an elaborate, shiny black beard. It looked like he'd had it permanent-waved in a beauty parlor. He also had a gold earring and was wearing a New York Yankees hat.

"Welcome to the finest shop in Manhattan," he said. "My name is Carlos Chatterjee.

If you don't see what you want, just ask. If I don't have it, I can get it for you in twenty-four hours."

In a large glass case, sort of like a freestanding wardrobe or closet, was an elaborate red suit of clothes, a tall kind of helmet-hat, and an old-fashioned musket. I had seen outfits like this before. I was about to ask a question, when Carlos Chatterjee came out with part of an answer.

"That item is NFS," he said. "Not for sale. It is the completely authentic in every detail grenadier's uniform belonging to a sergeant major in the 46th Regiment of Foot, under the command of the Honorable General John Vaughan, circa the year 1775. And it is my personal uniform."

"It's yours? That would make you a lot older than you look," Leni said.

"It's mine. I wear it to reenactments."

"Reenactments?"

"I am a reenactor, a Revolutionary War reenactor. We get together and act out famous battles. There are reeanactors who reenact battles of the Civil War, of the War of 1812. I happen to reenact battles of the Revolution. Some important ones happened right in this neighborhood: the Battle of Brooklyn Heights, Fort Washington, White Plains, Trenton, Princeton . . ."

"How about Kingston?" I asked.

"Oh, sure, the burning of Kingston, in 1777, my general, John Vaughan did that. Confidentially, he was a bit of a stinker. Us grenadiers did some bad stuff. I would rather have been an American troop, but this was the only uniform I could get. Yes, I've been to the burning of Kingston a few times. It comes around in October."

"Do lots of reenactors show up for that?" I asked.

"Maybe a dozen, it's not one of the biggies. We don't get to actually burn anything, or there would be a better turnout." Then he burst into song.

> Some talk of Alexander, and some of Hercules
> Of Hector and Lysander, and such great names as these.
> But of all the world's brave heroes There's none that can compare,

With a tow, row, row, row, row,
row, to the British Grenadiers.

We thanked Carlos Chatterjee for being so informative, and for the song, of course. Just to be polite we bought two of the cheapest items in the shop, a dollar forty-nine apiece for baseball hats printed with 86. STR., which, Carlos explained, stands for sechsundachtzigste Strasse, which means 86th Street. Carlos gave us cards that read, Das Kleine Museum/The Little Museum/El Pequeno Museo/Makumbusho Kidogo, and an address and phone number. We put on our hats and went down the stairs to my first subway ride.

19.

The New York City subway is a miracle and a monstrosity. It's a miracle because it can move huge numbers of people all around the city, safely, and in a short time. Our walk from 42nd Street to 86th Street had taken about forty minutes. The subway ride back took ten minutes. At going-to-work time and coming-back-from-work time, actual millions ride the subway. It's a monstrosity because it's far from clean, there are a great many smells underground, none of them nice, and it has rats. These are not like ordinary rats you meet in the woods, nice little animals going about their business. These are city rats, they're big and filthy, and they look you right in the eye.

While riding the subway, I thought I'd have to learn not to be afraid and disgusted by it when I moved to New York, which I would ultimately have to do in order to be near Papaya King. I looked at the faces of the other riders, and they seemed perfectly calm and happy, so obviously, it was possible to adjust . . . unless they had lost their minds from all the noise and funny odors, and weren't capable of realizing what an unnatural situation they were in.

On our way across town, we picked up a couple of slices from one of the pizzerias with a serving window open to the street. It's not that I was hungry, I was still riding the wave of satisfaction the papaya juice had created. I just wanted to compare New York City street pizza with Arnold Babatunji's. It stood up pretty well. Arnold's had more finesse, and was more like a work of art, but the slices (we held them folded, one-handed, and ate as we walked, like real New Yorkers) were not bad at all.

Adventures of a Dwergish Girl

Our bus was loading when we arrived at the ghastly Port of Authority, and I felt relief as I sank into the big bus seat. Finally, we were in a quiet place, and I realized I had not relaxed for a moment, or been without many kinds of stimulation all at once from the moment my sneakers hit the pavement.

The doors closed with a whoosh and a thunk, the little air vents whispered, and the bus lumbered forward.

20.

On the bus, Leni started in again. "About my aunt . . ."

"Oh yes, your aunt."

"Her name is Margaret, by the way."

"Aunt Margaret."

"She's a bit of a flake."

"Do tell."

"I mean, she's no one to trust with a confidence."

"Unlike you and me."

"Exactly. Anyway, Angus McMelvin, who is also unable to keep a secret, told her about the gangsters, and their plan."

"The plan to get hold of my gold."

"Well, not just yours, they believe the Dwergs have a whole big hoard of gold hidden away somewhere."

"This is correct. We've been stashing gold away since forever."

"Like in *Snow White*."

"I beg your pardon?"

"*Snow White and the Seven Dwarves*. The dwarves had a gold mine."

"That's right! I never made the connection before. I wonder if Walt Disney knew about Dwergs."

"Well, the gangsters know, and their plan is to follow you, or somehow find out where the Dwergs keep the gold, and take it all away."

"I'm not worried. It's a lousy plan."

"Why lousy?"

"Well, it would take a dumber than average gangster to assume that the Dwergs would not go to considerable lengths to hide all their gold. I mean, they wouldn't just keep it in bags in the closet, would they? Wouldn't they would keep it in a hiding place so clever that nobody living can find it?"

"How about somebody not living?"

"I assume you're referring to Leg Rhinestone, the ghostly gangster?"

"Among others. He has a couple of henchmen. Also, there are some living gangsters willing to hench for him."

"Well, the living ones can't find the gold. They can't even find the village, assuming that's where we keep the stuff. I suppose it just might be possible for ghosts, I wouldn't know, but since ghosts can't lift or carry material things, I'm not seeing a very serious problem. Of course, I suppose live gangsters might try to take away the gold I carry on my person, which amounts to two coins, but they'd have to be tougher than I am to get it, which I doubt."

"My Aunt Margaret says that Angus McMelvin says that the live gangsters, who are the ones he is friends with, say they have a way to do it. It's all figured out except for a few details."

"Such details being?"

"Well, the actual location of the hoard of gold is one, and then they need to time the theft with something that will distract everyone's attention while they make off with it. Apparently they've found out that the not-ghosts, not-dead, not-alive redcoats who've been seen around are going to do something distracting, such as set fire to the place. I don't know if they know that exactly, but they plan to use the redcoats as cover, or possibly get them to fetch the gold for them. The word is, as soon as the soldiers do something beside stand around eating disgusting things, they're going to follow them and watch for their chance."

"I'm finding it hard to take this seriously," I said. "It sounds like a goofy plan, but I am only a girl, and don't know all the answers. Unlikely as it seems, maybe Leg Rhinestone and the other no-goodniks have found a way to lay hands on the Dwerg geld. This might be the time for me to get advice from the ancient Dwerg, who is older and wiser than anybody else, and knows all the secrets from the beginning of our people."

"I think you should do that," Leni said.

"The only problem is we don't have an ancient Dwerg like that. The closest thing we have to a village wise man is my uncle,

Norbert, who knows all the ways there are to cook eggs, and is otherwise sort of an imbecile."

"So what are you going to do?"

21.

When I got back to Kingston it was already dark. Most of the shops on the block were closed. The lights were on in the pizzeria, and Arnold Babatunji and some policemen were standing around.

"What's going on?" I asked.

"What's going on is while you were in New York, I got held up," Arnold said.

"Held up?"

"Robbed, mugged, boosted, hijacked, knocked over, some guys in red uniforms came in and helped themselves."

"They took your money?"

"No, they took pizzas. You know the ones that are half-baked? I keep them on the counter, someone orders a slice, and I put it in the oven, finish baking it. They took those. They just muscled in behind the counter, grabbed all the pizzas, and walked out, munching. They never even said a word."

"Weird. And you called the police?"

"Of course I called the police, and you know what? These police tell me the exact same thing happened to my friend George Pafadopolis, who sells the horrible hot dogs. Same guys in the red suits, fished all the hot dogs out of the very hot water, and walked out eating them."

"When was that? About a week ago?" I asked. It had been about a week since I'd seen the redcoats on Frog Alley.

"Yes, a week."

"So what do you think it's all about?" I asked the policemen.

"It could be a crime wave," one policeman said.

"Or just a coincidence," another policeman said. "You know, some minor criminal types, who happen to all have red suits, just took some pizza without paying, which is a serious crime, of course."

"They all looked exactly alike," Arnold Babatunji said.

"How long were they here, would you say?" the policeman asked.

"Maybe a minute, maybe two, no longer than that."

"Hard to make a definite identification in such a short time," the other policeman said. "And you must have been surprised when they pushed behind the counter."

"Their faces were all the same," Arnold said.

"Well, if you should see them again, give us a call."

"Thank you, officers. And your pizza with bacon, sausage, peppers, mushrooms, eggplant, and olives is ready, please accept it as a tribute from a grateful merchant."

"We'll share it with the boys at the station. You are a fine citizen, Mr. Babatunji."

22.

"Billy Backus, I am appealing to you for help with a problem, because the closest thing to a Dwerg wise man now on earth is my uncle, Norbert, who, I say with no disrespect, is a drooling idiot."

"You understand that it has been a long time since I was a boy genius, and I may be out of practice."

"I only ask that you do your best."

"And no non-Dwerg knows much about Dwerg-lore."

"Not a problem. Dwergs themselves appear to have forgotten most of what they once knew. So you can't do much worse than Uncle Norbert, for example. Besides, I'm not sure this problem is exactly Dwergish."

"Then it's not about the bunch of gangsters, living and dead, who are planning to locate the fabled stash of Dwerg gold and make off with it."

"You really are Professor Knows Everything. The gangsters may figure in the story. I haven't quite decided yet, but mainly I want to go back to something we talked about before."

"The redcoats."

"Them. You expressed the opinion that they were not ghosts, and thus not dead, but also not alive. What could that mean?"

"Well, since we talked, I became curious, and looked a little further into the matter. I even found a few on the street late at night, and tried to talk with them."

"What was the result?"

"They don't talk much, or at all, but I did get a sort of rough idea of what they are."

"And what is that?"

"This may be difficult for you to grasp. They're unlike anything on the planet, as far as I know. Also, difficult to describe. I've been referring to them as meat-robots."

"You mean . . . ?"

"They're made of tissue, such as a living creature would have, but they're manufactured."

"Something like the Frankenstein monster?"

"Why didn't I think of that?"

"And the next questions would be, where did they come from, and why are they around here?"

"I can only guess, but I think it would not be too much of a stretch to suggest they are interplanetary, supernatural, or possibly from another plane of existence of which we are generally unaware. And as to what they're doing here . . ."

"I met a man in New York City who is a Revolutionary War reenactor."

"I think that may be what they're doing here."

"Reenacting."

"Instead of sentient individuals representing soldiers of the past, imagine a society with advanced technology, where some person or persons has or have an interest in history. They create these semi-alive, not exactly dead, creatures to be actors, or game-pieces, if you like, and carry out the historical events they're interested in. My guess is that children, or possibly childish men, on some other planet, or maybe an alternate plane of existence that normally doesn't connect with this one, are sitting in front of some kind of television screen, and watching what amount to animated chess pieces carry out their commands."

"So the bunch of replica redcoats, dressed in the uniform of the British 46th Regiment of Foot, from the last quarter of the eighteenth century, is here . . ."

"To reenact the burning of Kingston."

23.

"When you say 'reenact the burning of Kingston,' are we to assume they will actually set things on fire?"

"Well, their uniforms and the condition of their teeth suggest considerable attention has been paid to accuracy, so it might be reasonable to think they'll have authentic eighteenth-century torches when they get around to lighting the place up."

"You really think they're going to actually burn the place down?"

"I think it's likely. Of course, they may

just burn down the part they burned in 1777, that would be the Stockade District."

"That's the part we live in!"

"True. Someone ought to stop them."

"How? Who?"

"Can't help you very much with the how. As to the who, I think it's down to you."

"Me? Why me?"

"Well, at this moment, it's just us who have an idea of what's about to happen. I am more about theory, whereas you are very active, and a Dwerg. It will take someone pretty energetic to locate the only person who might be able to help with this."

"What person is that?"

"Witch."

"Which person, then. Why are you correcting my grammar at a time like this?"

"No, I mean the witch. The witch might help."

"Which witch are we talking about?"

"The Catskill witch."

"She's real? Nobody's ever seen her."

"She'll take some finding. See why it has to be you who does it?"

24.

It was nice that Billy Backus had such confidence in me, but how do you go about
witch finding? This wasn't just some garden
variety local neighborhood witch, either, it
was the Catskill witch, the one Dwergs tell
stories about, one that nobody has ever seen,
and it's not even sure that she exists. How
do you look for someone like that? Where do
you start?

I started at the public library. I had been
checking out books ever since I turned up
in Kingston, and took out a library card in

a false name. The librarian, Ms. Tieger, was nice, she suggested books, helped me look things up, and although it had not come up until now, she let me know that she could answer questions. I had a beauty of a question to ask her.

"Ms. Tieger, how would I go about finding a witch?"

"We have to narrow that down," Ms. Tieger said. "Would this be a witch in folklore or fiction?"

I said folklore for sure, but also this witch is thought to be real.

"There are people who practice the Wicca religion, and are considered witches. Would that be of any help?"

I told her I didn't think so. I explained I was looking for a witch in the locality, a witch with a reputation.

"There are a couple of garden-variety neighborhood witches, old ladies who visit the library, but I don't think that's what you're interested in, is it?"

"I need to find the Catskill witch," I said.

"And I am going to guess you do not mean the Catskill witch who fought in the

Revolution. In those days, witches were extremely unpopular, and they tended to get harmed by the community, but in her case, because she was such a deadly shot against the redcoats, no one complained about her."

"I read about her in one of the books you recommended," I said. "This witch is supposedly alive, at least I hope so. I need to meet with her."

"I'm going to have to go into the archive," Ms. Tieger said. "Come back to my office and have a cup of tea, you look as though you could use one."

Ms. Tieger had a cozy office in the back of the library. She put me in a big cozy chair, and made me a cup of tea with an electric kettle. I sipped the tea, which was lemony, while Ms. Tieger dragged thick dusty books off high shelves, unrolled bundles of what looked like old newspapers, and sat in front of a machine that showed microfilm images on a dim and fuzzy screen, and said things under her breath like, "Hmm," "Aha!," "Hum," and finally, "Eureka!"

"You found something?"

"I did! Here it is, the Yorkville witch."

"The Yorkville witch? But it's the Catskill witch I'm looking for."

"That's why I didn't find your witch right away," Ms. Tieger said. "The Catskill witch moved to Yorkville and is alive and doing business there!"

"Is this Yorkville a town, or the neighborhood in New York City?" I asked.

"The neighborhood. The witch's address is 361B East 86th Street."

"I was just there!" I said. "My friend and I went to Papaya King!"

"Two blocks from the witch's house on the corner of Third Avenue," Ms. Tieger said. "By the way, it says no appointment necessary, just ring the bell."

"This is the same witch who was known for years as the Catskill witch?" I asked. "She was considered a pretty big witch, powerful and unapproachable and all that. And now she's working out of a building on 86th Street?"

"Well, she has excellent reviews online," Ms. Tieger said.

"This is amazing," I said.

"You can get a lot done with libraries

and research," Ms. Tieger said. "People don't seem to know that. Instead of coming here with their questions, they talk to someone like Billy Backus."

I decided not to comment. Instead, I told the librarian I had to go sleep in a tree, thanked her, and left with a little slip of paper with the witch's address.

25.

I took an early bus, never realizing that it was going to hit Manhattan during rush hour. The bus was fairly full, and the passengers had grim expressions, but that didn't give me a clue of what was in store. What was in store, what I experienced from the moment I stepped off the bus, was organized madness. There were people in motion everywhere. Everybody was moving in a direction, purposely. They knew where they were going, and they were wasting no time in going there. I felt that if I stopped moving, if I stood still,

I'd be trampled to death, I had no choice but to move, and the waves and currents of people moved me in directions I had no intention of taking. I got swept along for a whole block sometimes, and it took a few corrections before I finally got myself onto 42nd Street, going east.

I took the subway! I didn't actually decide to take it, I just thought about it for a moment, wondered if I should go down and do it, and when I thought, I hesitated. I was standing near an entrance to the IRT Lexington line. The surge of people going down the stairs carried me with them. I didn't know where to buy a ticket or token, or whatever was called for, but it didn't matter, I was just carried onto the train. There were people crammed up against me! Bodies pressed to mine, front and back and both sides! There were times when my feet didn't touch the floor. The humanity thinned out a little as we rumbled uptown, and I was able to throw myself out the doors at 86th Street.

Most of the people using the stairs were going down and into the subway as I was trying to go up and out. I held onto the railings, scrambled with my feet, used my shoulders to push against people sometimes, and managed to drag myself up. It was hard work. When I got to the level of Carlos Chatterjee's store, and I saw the lights were on, I got myself unstuck from the torrent of down-stairsers, and went inside. I was panting and sweating.

"Hey, Molly!" Carlos said. "Back so soon!"

"Gotta catch my breath. Give me a minute," I said.

"I understand. Rush hour is a hustle, isn't it. I get the impression you haven't lived in the city very long."

"I haven't lived in it at all. This is only my second time being here."

"You're welcome to pull yourself together right here in my shop, after which, go down the street and get yourself a papaya juice, it's just what you need."

"I'll definitely do that. Meanwhile, just on a crazy impulse, may I ask you a question?"

"Certainly."

"Do you know anything about someone known as the Yorkville witch?"

"What a coincidence! That's my witch!

She lives just up the street, at 361B, in the back."

"She's your witch?"

"Yes, I go to her for advice, and spells, and communicating with my dead ancestors. I have to say, my tremendous success here in my shop has a lot to do with her help."

"So you are saying she's a good witch?"

"I am saying she's an outstanding witch."

"I mean, not a wicked witch."

"She's wicked good. I used to go to a witch all the way downtown, and she didn't do half as much."

"I'm on my way to see her."

"You won't be sorry."

26.

There was a little white card tacked above the bell-button, which said Witch. I pushed the button. A little white-haired lady opened the door. "By the Great Mother!" she said. "A Dwerg girl in New York City! Now I've seen everything! Come in, dear."

"I brought you a papaya juice," I said.

"How very kind!" the old lady said. "I will get glasses. Don't you agree that it's a little uncouth to drink from a paper cup when one is indoors?"

The apartment was small and tidy. The

furniture was old and worn-looking. There were framed pictures of butterflies on the walls.

"Sit here, dear, and tell me where you come from, and why you come to me. No, wait, let me guess . . . You're from that village of civilized Dwergs, with the goats and the goldmine, am I right?"

"You are," I said.

"Do you all still do that *latihan* thing where everybody hums?"

"We do," I said. "I didn't know that was what it was called."

"It's just my name for it, a Javanese word. I did my junior year abroad when I went to Sarah Lawrence. That's a college."

"I don't live in the village at present," I said. "I've been living in Kingston and working in a pizzeria."

"And are you getting on well, living with the English?"

"That is what I came to see you about," I said. "Not the English as in everybody who isn't us, but English soldiers from the days of the Revolution, only they're not, really. A friend of mine calls them meat-robots, and

we think they are going to reenact the burning of Kingston."

"That is clearly expressed, and succinct.
You're an intelligent girl. Interestingly
enough, a young man who comes to me for
witchcraft is a reenactor, but I don't think
he and his friends do any actual harm."

"Carlos Chatterjee, I've met him."

"Have you?"

"I have, and I would be interested in
whether you think he is an honest and
trustworthy person."

"I do. He is a fine young man, and a good
person to call on should you need help. He's
Hispanic and Hindu, it's a real New York
story. So, what did you want me to do about
these . . . let's not call them meat-robots, it
doesn't have a nice sound . . . Let's call them
androids."

"Well, stop them from burning down Kingston, or the oldest part of Kingston. Can
you do that?"

"I could do that, or you could do it. I would
help you, of course. Which do you prefer?"

"I have no idea how I would do it," I said.

"I will tell you what to do, and you will do

it. I think that is the best way."

"But you're the witch," I said. "Wouldn't it be better if you just handled it?"

"Have you ever considered that you might want to be a witch yourself someday? And even if you have not, saving a historic town from being consumed by flames would be quite an experience for a girl your age. It would give you confidence."

"I'm pretty confident by nature," I said.

"Good for you," the Catskill/Yorkville witch said. "Then it is settled. I will give you some hints, but not too many, and you will save the town."

"I feel a little dizzy," I said.

"Of course you do. Now sip your papaya juice while I work out how you're going to do this."

27.

"Before you get started, tell me how I should address you."

"Thoughtless of me, not to introduce myself. I am Lucinda Pannen. You may call me Mrs. Pannen, or Mevrouw Pannen."

"Meh-frow?"

"Close enough, it means Mrs., and what is your first name? I know you are a Van Dwerg."

I told her Molly.

"Just tell me, briefly, everything you know or have observed about these inflammatory infantrymen. Leave nothing out, but keep it short."

I told her, leaving nothing out, and keeping it short.

"Excellent. Now hush while I make a plan."

I hushed while Mrs. Pannen walked around the small living room with her hands behind her back. Occasionally she stepped on the cushions of an old sofa, and then onto the back, where she walked up and down like a cat. A couple of times she surprised me by jumping over an armchair like a sprinter clearing a hurdle.

A time or two, she stopped and looked at me with a strange, staring expression. "You said they ate disgusting frankfurters, and half-baked pizza, is that correct?"

I told her it was.

Finally she flopped into the armchair and patted her forehead with a lace-trimmed hanky. "That was invigorating," she said. "Now, in exchange for my telling you how to deal with the androidal arsonists, will you agree to follow my instructions, and also to give me what I ask in exchange?"

"Yes, I was going to ask you what kind of

fee. I have gold, and I can get more."

"Keep your gold. And, by the way, if you're talking about Dwergish coins, they're intensely valuable. Worth thousands apiece, I would imagine."

The thought crossed my mind that I should find time to do something very bad to Angus McMelvin.

"What I require in exchange for my witch-wisdom is that you carry out one final instruction when all the rest is done. Would you be willing?"

"What is the instruction?"

"When everything is accomplished, you are to leave Kingston. Clear out, and live someplace else."

"Well, I've been camping outdoors, and had already thought I'd be moving when the weather turns cold, and I was thinking about living in this very neighborhood."

"Because of the papaya juice, I expect," Mrs. Pannen said. "Of course, New York City is an exciting place to live, with many fine cultural opportunities, but I want you to live somewhere else for a while. I want you to go to Poughkeepsie."

"Poughkeepsie? But that place is a joke. Everyone makes fun of it. They say you'd have to be crazy to live there."

"There are often rivalries between nearby cities. No doubt Poughkeepsians make the same sort of jokes about Kingston."

"Do you think so?"

"Not really. But I want you to live there for a while anyway."

"Of course, I'll follow the advice of a famous witch, but may I ask why?"

"You know what destiny is, of course."

"Of course."

"Well, it is your destiny to be in Poughkeepsie in order for certain things to happen. You might say it is written."

28.

"This is what you must do. Find Oom Knorrig, tell him I sent you. Explain what you want to do, and ask if he will lend you the duck."

"Oom Knorrig? The duck?"

"Oom Knorrig is the old original Dwerg. You might call him the king of the Dwergs."

"We have a king?"

"Not as such, but Oom Knorrig, it means Uncle Grumpy, is the primary Dwerg. He is the living and hereditary example of what Dwergs were before they became the civilized, suburban Dwergs you grew up among, and felt the need to leave. He is a wild Dwerg. It will do you good to meet him."

"And the duck?"

"He has a duck."

"Where do I find Oom Knorrig?"

"I take it you're good in the woods."

"I am extremely good in the woods."

"Is there a part of the mountains where you've never been, and you can't remember planning to go?"

"Well, maybe . . . I suppose . . . not sure."

"That's the first thing you've not been sure about since you came in. You are not a not-sure sort of person. Could it be there's a direction, or an area, or a patch of the Catskills you are a tiny bit afraid of?"

"I'm not afraid of much," I said.

"Maybe just a little bit afraid, around the edges?"

"Well, there's a place with big trees that cast a lot of shade, so it's always dark, and the rocks are dark gray, almost black, and they stick up in an unusual way, and when I've gone in that direction there's always a cold wind."

"And what do you do when you approach that place?"

"It so happens that when I have approached that place, which has only been once or twice, it was just at the time I had already and previously decided I would turn back and go home . . . in order to arrive in time for lunch, that sort of thing."

"This time, take lunch with you. The place you describe is where you will start looking for Oom Knorrig."

"Would it be all right if I took a friend with me? I'm pretty sure she's good in the woods."

"Of course Leni may go with you."

"Oh, did I mention her name when I was telling you everything and keeping it short?"

"You must have, or how would I know it?"

29.

Before tackling the subway, I stopped into Carlos Chatterjee's shop. "Mrs. Pannen says you are a trustworthy person," I told him.

"I do my best," Carlos Chatterjee said.

"I'd like to ask you a question."

"Ask away."

"You deal in all sorts of odd merchandise, some rare and artistic stuff and some more on the funky-junky side."

"I consider it all rare and artistic, but I know what you mean."

"May I show you an item?"

"Certainly."

"Have you ever seen anything like this?"
I handed Carlos one of my Dwerg coins.

"Wow! I have not. But I have read about
and seen a drawing of such a thing. It is a
Dwergish coin, or maybe someone's idea of
what one would look like. They are probably mythical and don't really exist, but if
they did they'd be incredibly rare. May I ask
where you got it?"

"My father gave it to me."

"That's quite a gift." Carlos had whipped
out a tiny scale and put the coin on it. Then
he squinted at it through a magnifying thing
he stuck in his eye. "It's real gold, and worth
more than a thousand, that's just for the
metal in it. If it's old, and if it could be proven
to be real, it would be worth a whole lot."

"Is it something you would like to have?"

"I would love to have it, but it's worth
more than I can afford to pay."

"I'm not saying this will happen, but if it
were possible for you to earn this coin, would
you be interested?"

"Nothing against the law, of course."

"Of course."

"Then, yes."

"I have your phone number. If there is need, I will call you. It will be my first."

"Your first?"

"Phone call."

30.

"I was looking for you yesterday. I have a message to deliver," Leni Toomay said.

"I went to New York City."

"All by yourself?"

"Yep. I had a meeting with a witch. I'm going to tell you all about it."

"I want to hear, but before you do any telling, I have a piece of news and the message for you. The robot redcoats have struck again. This time they marched into the Knit Wit Shoppe, and ate skeins of wool."

"They ate wool?"

"They ate wool, a sweater, a scarf, and

some baby clothes, all knitted from wool, and the skeins, as I mentioned."

"That is unusual and disgusting," I said.

"It is. Now here is the message," Leni said. "Billy Backus says he wants to see you as soon as possible."

"I'll go see him right now," I said. "You come too. Meanwhile, are you up for a big hike in the woods?"

"Any time you like," Leni said. "I am good in the woods."

"To a scary part of the woods?"

"Even better."

Off to the side of Cows and Frogs, the shop run by Mrs. Backus, there is a door marked WKIN. Open the door, and there is a steep flight of stairs. Climb the stairs, go through another door, and you are in the radio studio. There's a sort of desk, with dials and lights, a record turntable, and various technical-looking gizmos and gimmicks. Sitting behind the desk, with earphones on, and a big microphone in front of his face, was Billy Backus. He held his finger up to his lips. Then he pointed to a couple of chairs. We sat down quietly.

"Time for some music on WKIN, it's the Hoosier Hot Shots recording of the beautiful and spiritual 'Ave Maria,'" Billy said into the microphone. Then he expertly put the needle at the edge of a record on the turntable, turned one big knob to the right, and then another big knob to the left. We heard the music leaking out of his earphones. "OK, girls, we can talk now," he said.

"You wanted to see me right away," I said.

"I do," Billy Backus said. "You know that some of those redcoated fellows hit the Knit Wit Shoppe, and ate the stock?"

"Yes, Leni told me about it," I said.

"And you recall that the same thing happened at Babatunji's pizzeria, and the horrible hot dog shop."

I said I did.

"You may find it interesting that I do advertising on the air for all three businesses. In fact, at the moment, they are my only advertisers. What does this suggest to you?"

"The radio station isn't doing very well?"

"That's just a temporary thing. I expect to get more sponsors. What I wanted to call to your attention was the fact that those eighteenth-century fleshopods only turned up at establishments belonging to advertising clients of mine. There are other restaurants in town they might have hit, and they ate wool, for Pete's sake, when there was a Boopsie Burger right next door. Does that suggest anything to you?"

"I know that Boopsie Burger," Leni said. "Given a choice, I'd eat the wool too."

"You're not picking up the important, and to a former boy genius, obvious, thing," Billy Backus said. "The ghastly grenadiers went to the places they went to because they heard the commercials I broadcast!"

"They listen to the radio?"

"That, or they are radios, or have a radio built in. I think they are given instructions by radio, and do what they are told when they receive them, and, if I'm right, the frequency on which I broadcast is the same, or close enough to, the one that they listen to for orders. They hear my ads, which usually include an imperative, like 'Go to Lonesome Cowboy Hot Wieners!' and then they do it."

"It's plausible," I said. "Interesting that,

weird and probably unearthly as they are, they're used to getting their orders in English."

"They're English soldiers."

"So they are."

"I thought I might devise a test or experiment using broadcast frequency, but I wanted to wait until I heard from you. Have you had any success in finding the Catskill witch?"

"Found her, and met with her yesterday," I said. I could see Billy Backus was impressed.

"And she advised you?"

"She did."

"Care to tell me what she advised?"

"She wants me to contact someone else. Have you ever heard anything about someone called Oom Knorrig?"

"Never, unless you mean the king of the wild Dwergs."

"You're a regular encyclopedia, Professor Knows Everything," I said.

"It's Oom Knorrig you're supposed to contact? Uncle Grumpy? I'm ninety-nine percent sure he's mythical."

"People say that about me," I said.

31.

Leni had spoken the truth—she was good in the woods. Of course, I had to slow down quite a bit, so she could keep up with me, but she kept a very decent pace for an ordinary human being.

"We're right outside my village," I said. "You can see the smoke from the chimneys."

"Where?" Leni said.

"I should have said, 'I can see it.' Maybe you can't. Look, if we climb up onto this rock, I can see the roof of my house."

We climbed up. "I can see trees," Leni said.

"Look between that big maple and the almost as big one." I pointed.

"Trees."

"No roof? No smoke?"

"Trees is all. Are you saying you can see that stuff?"

"Clear as can be."

"And I can only see trees?"

"That's how it's supposed to work."

"How does it work?"

"No idea, actually, and if you tried to walk to the village, you'd get turned aside without realizing it, whereas if I walked that way I'd go right in. We could try it if we had more time, but take my word for it."

"Makes you wonder what other things you can't see and other people can."

"And vice versa."

Starting from our location near my village, I knew just which way to go to arrive at that part of the forest I'd found a little bit . . . how shall I say? . . . potentially frightening. It wasn't very far, but it was uphill and rocky. As we got closer, the trees grew closer together and leafier, and blocked more and more light, there wasn't as much underbrush, and the bare earth was black and slippery. The temperature dropped, it was cool, then slightly chilly.

"What do you think of this?" I asked Leni.

"I can understand why my Native American ancestors made a point of not coming this way unless they had a very good reason. It's not like nature around here is hostile to us, more like it is indifferent to whether we live or die."

"That's how it feels to me," I said. "For example, look at how that bear is studying us." There was a black bear, sitting on his haunches fifty feet away. He was looking right at us, not afraid, not aggressive, not anything . . . We might have been a couple of birds on a branch.

Ordinarily, when I had encountered a bear it would act submissive or frightened, except in certain circumstances when it would warn me that it was protecting cubs, or was just in a bad mood. But I had never gotten this close to a bear that simply ignored me. I had slices of pizza in a knapsack, some for us to eat, and some as an offering to Oom Knorrig, and the bear must have smelled them, but he continued to show no interest when we came as close as twenty feet in passing him.

"Did that bear scare you?" I asked Leni.

"Nah, I know how to handle them, as I imagine you do too."

"Sure. I'm good with bears."

"How are you with really big fat rattle-snakes?" she asked.

"Oh, you mean like this one here? That is the biggest rattlesnake I have ever seen, it's as big around as my thigh! It must be really old."

"And have a ton of poison stored up," Leni said. "And look how un-snakey it's behaving."

It was like the bear, the snake was making no effort to get away from us, and also not coiling up, rattling, or being defensive. It was just going about its business as though we weren't there.

Something was becoming clear to me that I had never really given enough thought to, Dwerg that I am, and skilled as I may be in not making the least commotion in the woods, it is still a very different woods when no human is around. Everything that lives in the woods, all the birds and animals, and I'm going to guess plant life, too, is constantly aware and watchful when there are people present, even people like me. This makes sense if you consider the sort of things humans get up to. For some reason, the rules were suspended in this section of woods, and while we were uncomfortable because we didn't feel the rustle of fear and apprehension all around, as we had become used to, it was really the most peaceful place either of us had ever seen. We had just met two animals capable of killing us, and neither of them was even interested in us. What scared us a little, and apparently had scared Leni's ancestors, was that this was a place where humans were just another animal, not the top one. Once I got it, I began to like it. It was relaxing to feel like some bird, or bunny, or mushroom in the woods.

The angle of ascent got more acute, and sharp rocks stuck up toward the tree canopy, which was thicker, and blocked out more light. By now, we were mountaineering, or climbing rather than hiking, using our hands as well as feet to move along. Then we heard a voice.

It was the sweetest, cutest, most lovable voice we'd ever heard. And it spoke with an accent so adorable that we wanted to pick it up and stroke it, as though you could pet a voice. Ever since animated cartoons were invented, studios in Hollywood have hired voice actors who could make that kind of Kewpie-doll, Betty Boop, Elmer Fudd, Porky Pig sort of voice, but they had never found anyone who could produce sounds like we were hearing now.

"Who dares to approach the domain of Oom Knorrig, the horrible, the terrible? Bow to Oom Knorrig, and beg for your miserable lives!"

We could not help ourselves. "Awww," we both said.

32.

The moment we heard the sweet and delightful, cuddlesome little voice was the exact moment we'd stepped on a flat rock that rocked. It was a rocking rock. It just rocked a little, but that was enough to pull a string someone had attached to it, which string pulled a switch on an old-fashioned phonograph, the kind that didn't run on electricity, and had to be wound up with a crank. This phonograph we discovered seconds after being enchanted by the poopsie-woopsie, snuggly-wuggly, sweeter-than-sugar voice.

"It's a recording," I said.

"What do you suppose that is all about?" Leni asked.

"Possibly Oom Knorrig is so ghastly and frightening that he had some sweet-sounding type record the warning to stay out of his territory so people won't drop dead from fear."

"That sounds like a reasonable explanation to me," Leni said. "So what do you think we should do?"

"Well, I'm for going further into his territory, especially now that we're prepared to come across something ghastly and frightening."

"I agree," Leni said. "Forewarned is forearmed, and we have four arms between us. Let's wind up the phonograph for him, and reset the arm thingie, so it can scare the next victim."

"Good idea. Shows we're nice and helpful. We can tell Oom Knorrig we did that just before he eats us or chops us into little pieces."

The ground under our feet had turned more muddy. We tried not to slip as we followed an almost invisible trail. We felt reassured that we had not wandered off the path when we saw a signpost: Catskills Mountains Parsnip Festival This Way. It was faded and barely legible, the letters painted on rotting boards. There was another sign a little further along: Turn Back Or Die.

"I'm getting a little bored with this," Leni said. "Do you think we should start hollering for Oom Knorrig to show himself?"

"No need," I said. "Look what's up ahead."

"Talk about ghastly and frightening," Leni said.

Up the trail was a figure nobody could possibly fail to take seriously, or ever forget . ... maybe seven feet tall, or close to it, with a huge mop of tangled black hair, a gigantic nose, eyes of fire, a body completely disproportionate and knotty, with hands and feet like shovels.

"Wow. I am not disappointed," Leni said. "But isn't Oom Knorrig supposed to be a male?"

"That's how I've heard him referred to," I said. "But I suppose he can be anything he likes, and are you suggesting that we're looking at a female?"

144

"I'd say yes, technically," Leni said. "But what I'm more interested in knowing is whether we should run for our lives now."

"Oh, don't run away, now that you've come so far. Stay and have some roasted parsnips."

It was the voice we'd heard on the phonograph, and sitting on a tree stump was a person who was more than a match for it. This guy was cuter than a whole litter of kittens. It was all we could do not to throw our four arms around him.

"This is Hortense, my henchwoman," the little guy, who we were gratefully realizing was Oom Knorrig, and not likely to eat us or anything of the kind, said. "She does most of the henching around here, and is the most accomplished parsnip roaster in these mountains. I hope you will partake, not to do so would hurt her feelings."

I, personally, am partial to parsnips. In my opinion, they leave carrots in the dust, not that I have anything against carrots. Leni had somehow grown to advanced girlhood without ever encountering a parsnip, but she got the idea when Hortense handed her a tin plate of sliced ones, roasted to perfection.

We ate the parsnips with our fingers, making *Mmm!* and *Ahhh!* noises, while Oom Knorrig watched us beamingly, looking like the combined, never-realized dream of Walt Disney and every artist who ever worked for him. Hortense, I supposed, was showing us her pleasant expression, it was hard to tell, but the parsnips made up for a multitude of horribleness.

After the parsnips came tin mugs of blueberry tea. Oom Knorrig blew on his to cool it in an unbearably adorable manner and said, "Now, please refrain from telling me why you have come to see me. I know all about it already."

"You know all about it already? How is that possible?" I asked.

"I am Oom Knorrig, the horrible, the terrible. I know most things," he said, furrowing his brow and trying to look serious in a way that made us want to hug and kiss him. "Lucinda Pannen, also known as the Catskill witch, also known as the Yorkville witch, has sent you to me for help, is that not so?"

I saw Leni's hand move a little. Then she drew it back. I knew she had almost reached out to pinch the charming chubby cheek of the little darling Oom. I knew because I had the same impulse myself.

"I know you find me terrifying," Oom Knorrig said.

"Oh, no! Not at all! Not in the least! To the contrary!" Leni and I said.

"Yes, yes, you are very polite, and so is everyone I meet, but I know I am the last of the wild Dwergs, and strike fear into the hearts of all who meet me. So I will not prolong this visit."

"Please, prolong it! We could stay here forever," we said.

"Such good manners," Oom Knorrig said, in the sweetest way. "Since it will take hours and hours to explain what you must do to solve your problem, which I assure you I understand completely even though you have not devoted a single word to telling me about it, I will simply convey my wisdom to you by means of the waggle dance. Hortense! Get the bagpipes!"

"Wait a second!" I said. "The waggle dance? Like the bees do?"

"What an intelligent and well-informed

young woman!" Oom Knorrig said. "Yes, it is the same in principle, like the dance the bees do to tell the other bees the direction to fly when they have discovered a source of nectar. Hortense will provide the music, I will dance, you will follow me, and you will know exactly how to deal with the gigantic moose that's destroying your crops."

"Moose? Crops?"

"Your problem. Be assured, you will know the solution after we dance."

"It doesn't have to do with a moose," I said.

"Details. It will work or my name is not Oom Flanagan."

"We thought your name was Oom Knorrig."

"Consistency is the hobgoblin of small minds," the irresistible little wild Dwerg said.

33.

In case you've never heard of the wag-gle dance, also known as the dance of the bees, it's a real thing and well document-ed. A bee locates flowers, a source of nec-tar, goes back to the hive, and performs a complicated dance. The other bees observe and follow the dance, which in some way, not fully understood by science, tells them the direction and distance they need to fly. Studies have shown that much of the time, the bees are able to locate the nectar after watching and following the dance. A certain percentage of the time, they miss it. This could be because the bee communicating the details isn't such a good dancer, or the bees watching the dance don't pay attention. It's known as the waggle dance because the bee with the information does a lot of waggling his abdomen, which on a bee is the last part you'd see if the bee was flying directly away from you.

Oom Knorrig's human, Dwerg, or Dwerg-human, or Dwergish, or bee-ish waggle dance, we supposed, was meant to work along the same lines. Oom Knorrig's abdomen was in more or less the usual place for bipeds, so he waggled his completely adorable little heinie, which of course made Leni and me deliriously happy and joyous. We followed after, waggling our posteriors as best we could, wearing big smiles on our faces. Even Hortense's bagpipe playing, which was horrible, as we knew it would be, could not take anything away from the delightfulness of the dance.

I don't know how long the dance went on, it might have been an hour. We were warm and winded when Oom Knorrig stopped waggling, and we all sank to the ground.

"That went very well, I think," the last of the wild Dwergs said. "And I am sure you will have no more problem with the rotten eggs smell coming from your well."

"It's not about a well," I told the Oom.

"Well, your stream, brook, or rivulet, then, they're all much the same. And now, old Dwerg that I am, I'm a little fatigued after the dancing, and need to curl up for a nap among a lot of daisies."

We pictured the darling little fellow napping surrounded by flowers, and were mentally saying, "Awwww!" when he vanished into thin air.

"OK, girls, you have been assisted by Oom Knorrig, the uncrowned king of the Dwergs," Hortense said. "If you have a complaint, tell us, if you're satisfied, tell your friends. Here is a large parsnip for each of you. The duck will show you the way, now get out of my sight."

It was a large white duck. It led us to the rocking rock, which we were perfectly capable of finding without help, and we were back on the trail again, heading for home.

"Don't you just love him?" Leni asked me.

"I so do," I said. "And how about that dancing?"

"The dancing was fantastic," Leni said. "I don't remember ever dancing so much."

"And Hortense is scary, but I think she's nice deep down," I said.

"She does good parsnips," Leni said. "So do we know what to do about the planned torching of Kingston, and the attempt to steal the Dwerg gold?"

"It doesn't feel as though I do," I said. "But I have some great ideas about how to deal with a renegade moose."

34.

Being dead is not all it's cracked up to be. If you're a spirit of the departed, you can't eat anything, you can't really do anything, about all you can do is know things, and what's the good of knowing things if you can't tell anybody?

"Say, do you know what's next week?" Roger Van Tussenvuxel asked me.

"What's next week?" I asked him.

"October 16th, that's what's next week."

"OK, so October 16th happens next week. Why is that something?"

"It's an anniversary, October 16th, 1777. The burning of Kingston."

"Oh. So, if someone was going to reenact . . ."

"Stands to reason."

"So it does, but do not worry. I have it all taken care of."

"You do?"

"Yes, Roger, I do. You expect that the re-enacted burning of Kingston, or anyway the part of Kingston that got burned in 1777, was going to be carried out by those dead-and-alive British soldiers who've been seen around lately, is that not so?"

"Well, yes, that is the word among us departed."

"But you did not know, and apparently no other ghost knew, that I made a deal with those troops."

"You did? I heard nothing about it."

"I am arranging for a distinguished military man, a noncommissioned officer, to lead them to the secret hiding place of the vast hoard of Dwerg geld. They will remove the many bags of gold and take them to a safer location. So you see, nothing will happen to the gold when they set fire to the city, and all is well."

"But they are still going to set fire to the city?"

"Well, yes, but we have a modern fire department now, and you, more than most, will remember the town was rebuilt after the last time. The gold will be safe, that's the important thing . . . Not that it was in much danger in the cave, but you never know, fires get out of hand, there might be a collapse or something."

"The gold is in the cave? The Kingston Cave?"

"Yes, no harm in telling you. It won't be there much longer. Besides it's way deep in the cave, very unlikely anyone could find it. The soldiers will be marched to it, pick it up, and *snip-snap-snoo*, the deal is done. Just the same, you'd better not tell anyone."

"No, of course not."

"Mum's the word. *Shtoom! Schweig! Silencio!*"

"Wow. You'd have thought some ghost would have known about this." Roger was impatient to get away from me so he could start telling other ghosts that he knew something they didn't. He had fallen for it like a ton of weightless bricks.

35.

Arnold Babatunji showed me how to punch the numbers on his phone.

Ring ring ring . . . "With a tow row row row row row, Carlos here, how may I help you?"

"You can help me by turning up in Kingston with your full uniform no later than tomorrow. It's Molly, by the way, speaking via telephone. There's a Dwergish coin in this for you."

"You don't have to pay me. I am happy to help."

"No, no, I want you to have the coin. Oh,

and look around your shop and see if you have any moose repellant."

"What? Moose repellant?"

"Did I say that? Never mind. Just bring yourself, and the uniform. You don't have to wear it on the bus. Ask anybody where to find Babatunji's pizzeria. Wait for me there."

"Will I need the musket?"

"No, no musket needed."

"Sword?"

"A sword might get in the way."

"How about a flag? I have a number of flags."

"You'll be carrying something other than a flag. You're pretty strong, aren't you?"

"I do 18th-century British Army calisthenics every morning."

"Babatunji's pizzeria. I'll see you tomorrow."

36.

"Molly? I thought you were living among the English in Kingston, and working in a pizzeria."

"I am, most of the time, Uncle Norbert, but I came back to the village to see you about a special subject."

"Is there such a thing as a scrambled eggs pizza? You know, it is generally thought that I know all the ways there are to prepare eggs, but I always worry there might be one I haven't heard about."

"As far as I know, such a pizza does not exist, but I think it is a good idea. I am fairly sure I can get my employer, Arnold Babatunji, to put it on the menu, and it can be called the Pizza Norbert in honor of the inventor . . . that would be you. You can come to the shop and be served the very first one ever to exist."

"I am a bit shy to come to a pizzeria in a town."

"Then I will bring you one. I will run all the way, and get it to you piping hot."

"You are a fine niece, niece."

"Will you do a small favor for me?"

"If I possibly can, I will."

"I believe you are known and admired for your skill in making Catskill Mountain juniper juice, also known as Dwergish gin."

"I am, but what interest could a child like yourself have in it?"

"I need a large keg of it."

"Niece, that stuff is dynamite. It is not for children, or adults even. Even most Dwergs won't touch it."

"It is not for me to drink, but I have a very good reason to ask for it."

"I have a keg. It has been aging for two weeks, and is ready for consumption, but

I am hesitant lest it fall into the wrong hands."

"I promise it will be used in a good cause. And I would never do anything that would even indirectly bring dishonor to my uncle, let alone the inventor of the Pizza Norbert."

"You are an honest child, and I trust you, but a keg is rather heavy. I'm not sure you can carry it very far."

"I have arranged for a strong fellow to carry it. Will you leave it behind the ancient oak tree outside the village?"

"You know, this is the stuff they gave to . . ."

"I am familiar with the story."

37.

"You know those big parsnips Hortense gave us?" It was Leni talking. "You didn't eat yours or anything?"

"No, I've still got mine, and I know what you're going to say."

"I think mine may be a magic parsnip. I discovered something about it last night."

"So did I. If you're in a very quiet place, and you yourself are very quiet, and you listen carefully, the parsnip will talk to you."

"So it's not just mine, it's . . ."

"Both of them."

"Mine picks up voices, conversations going on somewhere else."

"Like a radio."

"Yes, only I think these are ghostly conversations."

"That's what I think too. And what are the ghosts talking about when you hear them on your parsnip?" I asked Leni.

"They're all excited. They're talking about how the Dwerg gold hoard is way deep in the Kingston Cave, and the fleshopoidal soldiers are going to remove it, and then they're going to set fire to the town."

"Did you pick up any conversations involving ghostly gangsters?"

"I was saving that for last. I heard someone who could only be Leg Rhinestone, talking with his henchmen, alive and dead. They intend to follow the soldiers, see where they move the gold, and then steal it. The live ones will do the actual henching, and the ghostly ones will sort of encourage them and supply brainpower, such as they've got."

"All of this is just what we wanted to happen. It's some plan, isn't it? I wonder if we actually thought it up, or whether we got it from doing the waggle dance with Oom Knorrig."

"I'm going to say it's because of Oom Knorrig, because he's so darn cute."

"Now we have to see Billy Backus, and make sure he understands what he has to do," I said. "And I'd better go and see Mr. Winnick."

"Who's Mr. Winnick?"

"Someone," I said. "He does things for the Dwergs. I'm a Dwerg and I need him to do some things for me. Then we wait for Carlos Chatterjee to show up. Oh, and I have to take a scrambled eggs pizza to my uncle. I think that's everything for the moment."

38.

Mr. Winnick had a little office right across
from the old courthouse. Everything in
the place was made of dark wood, the walls, the
ceilings, the furniture, and it was all crackled
and ancient-looking. It looked like nothing had
changed in two hundred years. Mr. Winnick
looked like nothing about him had changed
in two hundred years. He was a fat man, with
no neck, and his fat little hands were folded
on his fat stomach. He was jammed behind
his two-hundred-year-old desk.

"No need to tell me your name, Miss Van
Dwerg," Mr. Winnick said.

"I don't know if that means you know who I am, or just can see that I'm a Dwerg," I said.

"You're not meant to know, and I must tell you that I do not wish to hear any secrets. Also, if I am asked who came to see me this day, I will say a Miss Van Dwerg, member of a very large family, who did not tell me her first name, or her address. Do not tell me your address."

"Am I allowed to tell you why I came here, and what I hope you can do for me?"

"If you mention no names. As to doing something for you, it is my honor and my responsibility to do anything within the law for anyone of your last name, and I have at my disposal virtually unlimited funds, should they be needed."

"Then I will tell you my plan," I said.

"Do so, but do not tell me any plans," Mr. Winnick said. "Rather tell me an interesting story you are making up in your head as you go along. If asked, I will say that a certain Miss Van Dwerg visited my office and told me a story for purposes of amusement."

I told Mr. Winnick my story.

"A very good story, Miss Van Dwerg," Mr. Winnick said. "You should write a novel. Apropos nothing, I mention to you, completely out of context, and for no earthly reason, that I have excellent relations with the police, and other city departments, and getting a necessary permit at the last minute would be no problem for me, not that I needed to tell you that."

"I understand," I said. "You are just making idle conversation."

"Correct," Mr. Winnick said. "As to many other aspects of your story, I should say part of its charm is the fact that such things could very well happen in real life."

"I have something to add, not part of my story, as such."

"Proceed."

"Would it be possible to acquire a secret, patent-protected, papaya-juice juicing machine from the Papaya King, and have it delivered to Arnold Babatunji, the pizza-maker?"

"I know the King personally," Mr. Winnick said.

39.

Carlos Chatterjee was a strong and energetic guy. After putting the heavy keg he'd carried all the way from the woods in Billy Backus's radio studio, he bounded down the stairs and sprinted to the pizzeria to get the duffel bag containing his uniform, which he'd stashed there.

Billy opened a door connecting to a tiny apartment. "Make yourself at home, Carlos," he said. "Feel free to have a bath, take a nap. Would you like something to eat?"

"I had two large mushroom pizzas a while

ago," Carlos said. "And I brought some comic books with me. I'll be fine."

"Conserve your energy," Billy said. "The balloon goes up at eight o'clock."

"There's going to be a balloon?"

"Figure of speech. You go rest now. I'll let you know when to put the uniform on."

Leni and I were sitting in the visitors' chairs in the studio. "This next part is the critical one," I whispered.

"What if it doesn't work?" Leni whispered back. "What do we do then?"

"Then we buy bags of marshmallows, and get ready to roast them over the flames of old Kingston."

"So the whole business depends on Billy Backus?"

"He's a former boy genius, I have confidence."

Billy made a throat-cutting gesture with his hand, which is the radio studio signal to be quiet, and turned the big knob. Then he produced a toy trumpet from under the console and blew a few notes. "Soldiers of the king!" he said into the microphone in a commanding voice. "Assemble tonight at eight in front of the Cows and Frogs Gift Emporium, your source for tasteful crafts and works of art featuring the popular cow, and the beloved frog. Bring your torches. You will report to Sergeant Major Chatterjee, and obey his orders. Button up your tunics, blow your noses, put your headgear on straight." Then he blew a few more notes on the toy trumpet.

"Think that will work?" I asked Billy Backus.

"I see no reason it shouldn't."

"Are you going to repeat the announcement?"

"Either they got it or they didn't," Billy said. "Did you do everything we talked about?"

"I went and saw Mr. Winnick."

"And he said he'd handle things?"

"He didn't say anything definite."

"Well, nothing to do but wait and see what happens," Billy Backus said. He pulled a folder out of a sort of bookcase for long-playing phonograph records, and slid two discs out of it. "Symphony Number 3, by Gustav Mahler," he said. "Takes about an hour and a half. Then I'll tell Carlos to put the uniform on."

It was nice music. Leni and I gradually slid out of our chairs and fell asleep, curled up on the carpet. Billy Backus leaned back in his radio announcer's chair and snored quietly.

40.

"Wake up, girls, the symphony is finished," Billy Backus said.

Carlos Chatterjee had put on his Sergeant-Major-in-the-British-46th-Regiment-of-Foot-circa-1775, uniform, complete with boots and tall pointy hat. He looked good. The big clock on the wall showed it was 7:55 P.M. The studio was soundproof, but I thought I could hear drums outside.

Leni ran downstairs and opened the door. The sound of drumming got louder. It wasn't a military rhythm. "That sounds sort of like a calypso beat," I said.

"It's actually *mento*," Billy Backus said. "Which is similar to calypso, but comes from Jamaica, whereas calypso comes mostly from Trinidad."

"You'd better come down and see this," Leni called up the stairs.

There was quite a lineup of people in the street. First there were four adorable children holding a banner that read, Kingston, New York Salutes Kingston, Jamaica. Behind the children were the androidal flesh-robot redcoats, each holding a torch. Behind the torch-bearers were *mento* musicians with drums and banjos and trumpets, and dancers wearing some pretty fancy costumes, with a lot of feathers and bright colors.

It seems there are a fair number of people from the island of Jamaica living in Kingston, and others from different places in the Caribbean. Others have no personal connection with the islands, but they just like them, and apparently some of them possess costumes, or can play music. Somehow Mr. Winnick had gotten word to everybody to come and take part in the Kingston Honors Kingston nighttime parade.

Carlos Chatterjee, with the keg on his shoulder, took his place at the front of the line, and barked some orders at the troops. They snapped to attention. Then he told them to light their torches. They took out Zippo lighters and did so. Then Carlos lifted the arm that was not steadying the keg on his shoulder as though he held an imaginary sword, and shouted, "Forward! March!" The soldiers stepped off smartly, holding their torches in the air.

The drummers drummed, the players played, the dancers twirled and strutted, and the whole combination moved off down the street, and turned left at Broadway. We marched alongside on the pavement. Kingston policemen, stationed at the intersections, held up traffic as the parade passed by.

A little distance behind, three or four guys in greasy double-breasted suits followed along. They looked like gangsters, which of course they were.

41.

The people of Kingston had finished their suppers, and were watching television, or playing a game of cards at the kitchen table, or just sitting on the steps of their houses, enjoying the evening air. They heard the drums and the playing and singing, they saw the light of the torches, and they came forward to have a look.

I have to say, I was proud of the Kingstonians. They applauded the music and the dancers, and they insulted and objected to the soldiers with torches.

"Phooey!" they shouted. "Go home, lobster-backs!" "Down with the redcoats!" "We don't like torchlight parades!" and "No taxation without representation!" I doubt they even knew the intention of the troops with the torches was to burn the place down, they just didn't like the image.

The music was good, and lots of people marched along Broadway with the parade, like we were doing. There was a lot of cheering and clapping and hollering, and some of the citizens joined the dancers and became part of the show.

When the parade, and the crowd that was going along with it, came to Wurts Street, where there's a little park, we saw that the lights on the baseball diamond had been turned on, and what should be there, at home plate, but the Papaya King mobile unit? I say we saw it, but we smelled the hot dogs, tastier than filet mignon, first. And there was a flashing electric sign on top of the mobile unit: Free!

The parade and the onlookers dissolved into a seething mob of happy people munching hot dogs and experiencing papaya juice.

Except the redcoats. They remained in formation and under orders. Carlos marched them off in the direction of the Rondout Creek. The gangsters shuffled after.

"May I offer you a papaya juice?" I asked Leni.

"Why not?" Leni said. "And isn't Carlos doing a perfectly splendid job?"

"He is. He's getting two Dwergish coins after this night's work."

"Shall we stroll down to the cave and be in at the finish?"

"Yes, let's." And sipping our juices, we strolled.

42.

By the time we reached the entrance to the cave, Carlos was emerging, holding one of the torches.

"It can't be over already!" I said.

"Over and done with," Carlos said. "It was easy."

"Tell us everything!"

"Well, first I marched my troops all the way down in the cave. This is some cave, it goes on and on. When I found a nice dry area, that looked like nobody has been there in decades, I had them unroll their regulation blankets and sit down in a neat row along the wall, tucked up nice and warm. Then I ordered them to take out their tin cups, and I poured everyone a drink from my keg. The gangsters who'd been following us had come in close, probably expecting we were near the gold, so I offered them drinks too. They didn't have tin cups, but I had some Dixies in my knapsack, it wasn't historically authentic, but sometimes you can't help it. Then we all drank a toast to the king. I didn't drink, of course. Then they all went to sleep, and I left them there, snoring happily. As I understand it, they'll wake up in twenty years, like old Rip."

"You know, Carlos, when I first met you, a nice enough fellow, but really just a shopkeeper on 86th Street, I would never have guessed that you'd wind up being the hero of the story."

"You can't tell how things will work out, and it was my pleasure to be of use."

"What I'm wondering now," Leni said, "is what happens when they wake up twenty years from now. Will they still be programmed to do arson?"

"If you guys are still in the neighborhood when that happens, you'll know how to deal with it," I said. "As for me, it won't be my problem. I have to leave this place now."

"You're leaving?" Leni asked. "Where will you go?"

"Poughkeepsie."

"Poughkeepsie? You'll go nuts in that town! Why there?"

"A witch told me it was my destiny."

About the Author

DANIEL PINKWATER is the author and sometimes illustrator of more than one-hundred (and counting) wildly popular books, including *The Neddiad*, *Lizard Music*, *The Snarkout Boys and the Avocado of Death*, *Fat Men from Space*, *Borgel*, and the picture book *The Big Orange Splot*. He has also illustrated many of his own books, although for more recent works that task has passed to his wife, illustrator and novelist Jill Pinkwater. Pinkwater is an occasional commentator on National Public Radio's *All Things Considered* and appears regularly on NPR's *Weekend Edition Saturday*, where he reviews kids' books with host Scott Simon. Pinkwater also contributed to *Wondertime*, and has in the past been spotted on the pages of the *New York Times Magazine*, *OMNI*, and many other publications.

Pinkwater lives with his wife and several dogs and cats in a very old farmhouse in New York's Hudson River Valley.

About the Illustrator

AARON RENIER is the author of three graphic novels for younger readers: *Spiral-Bound, The Unsinkable Walker Bean,* and *The Unsinkable Walker Bean and the Knights of the Waxing Moon.* He is the recipient of the Eisner Award in 2006 for Talent Deserving of Wider Recognition, and was an inaugural resident for the Sendak Fellowship in 2010. Renier teaches drawing and comics at universities in Chicago